NEW YEAR, NEW GUY

When Polly organises a surprise re-union for her fiancé and his long-lost American friend, her sister, Laura, grudgingly agrees to help keep the secret. And when the plain-spoken, larger-than-life Hunter McQueen steps off the bus in her rainy Devon town and only just squeezes into her tiny car, it confirms that Laura has made a big mistake in going along with her sister's crazy plan. But could the tall, handsome man with the Nashville drawl be just what Laura needs to shake up her life and start something new?

D1610579

NEW YEAR, NEW GUY

When Polly organises a surprise reunion for her fiancé and his long-lost American friend, her sister, Laura, grudgingly agrees to help keep the secret. And when the plain-spoken, larger-than-life Hunter McQueen steps off the bus in her rainy Devon town and only just squeaks into her easy, it confirms that Laura has made a big mistake in going along with her sister's crazy plan. But could the tall, handsome man with the Nashville drawl be just what Laura needs to shake up her life and start something new?

ANGELA BRITNELL

---◆---

NEW YEAR, NEW GUY

Complete and Unabridged

LINFORD
Leicester

First published in Great Britain in 2020 by
Choc Lit Limited
Surrey

First Linford Edition
published 2021
by arrangement with
Choc Lit Limited
Surrey

A catalogue record for this book is available
from the British Library.

ISBN 978–1–4448–4685–0

Published by
Ulverscroft Limited
Anstey, Leicestershire

Set by Words & Graphics Ltd.
Anstey, Leicestershire
Printed and bound in Great Britain by
TJ Books Ltd., Padstow, Cornwall

This book is printed on acid-free paper

Dedication

To the wonderful ladies in the Technical Services Department of the Williamson County Public Library in Franklin, Tennessee without whose behind-the-scenes hard work there would be no books on the shelves (including mine!) and a lot of unhappy patrons.

Acknowledgements

I've been looking for the right book to include the beautiful area of Dartmoor in Devon and Laura and Hunter's story handed me the ideal opportunity. This plain-speaking, no frills couple fell in love with the stark beauty of this stunning National Park in winter as they fell for each other. Mission accomplished.

Huge thanks to the Tasting Panel members who agreed with me that Hunter fitted the mould of the perfectly irresistible Choc Lit hero and wanted to give him and Laura the happy ending that they totally deserve: Mel R, Isabelle D, Gillian C, Karen M, Kirsty T, Jo O, Gill L, Carol D, Cordy S, Gillian H and Anne E.

1

A trickle of freezing rain slid down the one centimetre gap between Laura's upturned collar and her bare neck. This was why no one except her half-baked sister risked getting married in the middle of dismal January in soggy Plymouth instead of planning a destination wedding somewhere hot and tropical.

Picture a winter wonderland. Think of the church fragrant with paperwhites and glowing with creamy white roses and tulips intermingled with pops of yellow forsythia.

She stamped her feet in a desperate effort to return some trace of feeling to her toes. If this idiot didn't arrive she'd give Polly a piece of her mind. *No you won't.* What Laura owed her sister couldn't be paid back if she stood in the pouring rain for a month. Through the fading afternoon light a bus pulled into

1

the bay in front of her and shuddered to a noisy halt.

A few seconds later she understood why Polly smiled when she'd asked for a picture of Hunter McQueen.

Trust me, according to the way Johnny always describes him, you won't be able to miss the man.

Laura spotted a huge man towering above the group of passengers who piled off the bus.

'Yeah, thanks, but I'm good for a ride.' A deep voice laced with a thick American drawl boomed out. 'Some cute British babe's picking me up.'

Gritting her teeth in a weak smile she walked across to him. 'Mr McQueen?' An amused grin rested on her, all white teeth and mischievous sky-blue eyes. 'I'm —'

' — Miss Laura Williams. My saviour.'

Engulfed in an unexpected hug she was trapped against the broadest, hardest chest she'd ever come into contact with and inhaled the man's warm woodsy scent. Anyone would think he'd spent

2

the day chopping down trees instead of being crammed in an overheated bus all the way from London.

'Tiny little thing, aren't you?'

Finally she managed to wriggle loose. 'How was your journey? I'm surprised you chose the bus when the train's far quicker and a lot more pleasant.'

'I like bus people.'

'Bus people?'

'All sorts of people ride buses and most are up for talking.'

Five hours trapped next to a talkative stranger would be her idea of hell. 'Have you got your luggage yet? I think the driver's taken everything out.'

'It's all here.' He hoisted a camou-flage backpack on one shoulder.

'That's it?'

'Yep. I'm a plain kind of guy all around. Take me as you find me.'

'I'm the same . . . although not the guy part.'

'Obviously.'

Laura suspected complete honesty with this man would be a terrible idea.

Hunter McQueen was Polly's wedding surprise for her fiancé. The appearance of Johnny's old friend should be the highlight of Saturday night's party. The engaged couple had decided it wasn't modern to hold separate hen and stag dos which was why everyone was meeting at their favourite Greek restaurant for an evening of great food, lashings of ouzo and the obligatory plate smashing. Laura's assignment was to keep Hunter McQueen out of the way until the party. She'd briefly wondered if this was a matchmaking attempt on her sister's part but no way would Polly attempt to pair her off with this garrulous man.

'Follow me,' she said, and sighed to herself. This promised to be a long three days.

★ ★ ★

'Mr McQueen, this is mine.' The brisk statement stopped him seconds away from walking right past a miniature bright blue car.

4

'For a start let's ditch the whole Mr McQueen bit and stick to Hunter.' A layer of reticence shadowed her eyes and he wondered what lay behind Laura's wall of quiet good manners. He eyed up the tiny vehicle. 'Do you have a shoehorn?'

'Polly didn't warn me you were . . . '

' . . . oversized?' Despite the late afternoon darkness closing around them Hunter sensed her heated blush.

'I wouldn't quite say that!'

'I would.' Hunter laughed. 'I shop at big and tall stores, bump my head on low hanging lights and wish I was a good six inches shorter on most airplanes. Even a polite Brit can't phrase it any other way.'

She gestured towards the front passenger seat and he obediently folded himself into the narrow space and buckled his seat belt. Before she managed to suppress it a fleeting glimpse of amusement pulled at her mouth sending an unwanted tingle of interest shooting through him. No one would label Laura as beautiful.

The slightly too long nose, a narrow face at odds with her soft curvy body and a wide mouth that worked on Julia Roberts but not so much on this woman. He hadn't yet nailed the colour of her eyes but suspected they might be a muddy-brown shade.

'My home's about twenty minutes away in Crownhill. You'll stay out there with me until the party and Polly said you'd be doing your own thing after that until the wedding.'

'That's kind of you, ma'am but I can make myself scarce now if it suits you better.'

'Pleasing Polly suits me better. She asked me to take care of you and that's what I'll do.' Her grim determination made it almost impossible not to laugh, but she'd take it the wrong way. 'I'm sorry. I didn't mean to sound — '

' — No beating around the bush, right? It's all good.'

'Have you visited this part of the country before?'

'No.' He kept the answer short

6

because too many details would stir up questions he'd no intention of answering. When he stepped onto English soil this morning for the first time in twenty years it had all flooded back. The grim brutality of Greystone and everything connected to the London school where he spent two long years. Danny Pearce's thin pinched face when Hunter betrayed him. Hunter's complicated relationship with Johnny Matthews. All of these things had shaped his adult life but they definitely weren't something he intended on discussing with this woman. 'When I'm on the lookout for a change from Nashville I prefer to soak up the sun on a hot, white, sandy beach with a strong rum drink in one hand.'

'And a beautiful girl in the other?'

'You got a problem with that? I'm single and my New Year's resolution last week was to stay that way.' Hunter grinned. 'I've made the same promise every year since Mary Lou Kowalski broke my heart in eighth grade.'

'She must've been special.'

'Oh yeah she was that all right. Without being crass let's say she . . . developed before any of the other girls and made the most of her assets.'

'I assume she didn't know you existed?'

'She knew all right.' He chuckled. 'Mary Lou granted me one heart-stopping kiss after the Christmas school dance and promised much more the next day.' Hunter shook his head. 'Didn't sleep a damn wink that night I can tell you but in the morning she cut me dead in the hallway. In the cafeteria at lunch she was draped around Troy Madden, handsome quarterback on the football team and prize jerk.'

'That's life.'

The grim set of Laura's jaw hinted he'd strayed into dangerous territory. 'What resolution did you make?'

'None.' She scoffed. 'If people don't have the willpower to diet, give up smoking or stay single without an idiotic public promise it's not going to happen.'

'Wow. You cut to the chase, don't you?'

8

'I thought that was your philosophy too?'

He'd suspected he'd been hoist on his own petard, whatever one of those even was.

'Anyway, believe it or not, it's beautiful around here when it isn't raining.'

'If there's a set day of the year that happens I might make a point of coming back.'

She tossed a brief smile his way before turning down a street of unremarkable, older houses.

'Why are they divided up that way?' He couldn't help comparing the drab identical homes to the modern, custom-designed log cabins he built back in Tennessee.

'Because a semi-detached house gives the impression of living somewhere much larger while being much more affordable.' Laura pulled her car into a narrow gravel driveway and killed the engine. They both got out, although it took more effort on Hunter's part. 'That only works if the two sides choose the same paint colour.' Her eyes gleamed and Hunter followed her gaze to register a bright red door on the right and solid black on Laura's side. 'See what I mean?'

'Yep, it'd be kind of hard to pull off in your case.'

'Most things are.'

Her muttered words pulled him up short. Any interest he might have in this woman was a bad idea.

'Lead the way.' Hunter wiped his boots on the mat and followed her inside.

In three days he'd do the surprise thing at the party — although he'd bet his bottom dollar Johnny wouldn't be as thrilled as his fiancée expected — and then make immediate tracks back to Tennessee. He didn't plan on hanging around another week for the big day, but if he shared that with Laura now she would feel obliged to pass the news on to her sister.

He glanced around the small square hall. 'Nice place.'

She threw him a vaguely suspicious

look and Hunter plastered on his most amenable smile. Laura was too quick on the uptake to fool for long.

2

Laura gestured towards the stairs. 'You can take your things up while I put the kettle on. Your room's the second on the right next to the bathroom.'

'Thanks. Have you lived here long?'

'I bought it about two years ago after — sorry, I'd be happy to stand here talking, but I'm freezing and dying for a cup of tea.'

A flash of curiosity niggled at him. 'I could've got a cab from the bus station.'

'Not according to my sister.' Laura shook her head. 'Her instructions were most specific.'

'What's Polly like?'

'Like?'

'Yeah. Just wondering what sort of girl old Johnny's getting hitched to.'

'The best.'

Her instant defence made him smile.

'I'm sure she is. I'll leave you to your tea making.'

Hunter sprinted up the stairs and grimaced when he opened the door. His house had closets larger than this. He tossed his bag on the narrow single bed. Its only redeeming feature was the lack of a footboard meaning he could at least hang his feet off the end. The room was a study in drabness from the beige walls to the brown velvet curtains and dark mahogany furniture. A sparse break from the bland colour palette came in the form of a couple of innocuous framed landscapes. It all reinforced his first impression of this being an investment rather than a real home.

Tugging off his boots he stretched out on the bed and a sluggish tiredness gnawed away at him.

A loud bang jolted Hunter awake and his jagged heartbeat thundered against his chest. Back at home he always left his bedroom door ajar but here that wasn't possible without arousing Laura's suspicions. He'd forgotten to open the window instead and was paying the price. The familiar layer of nervous sweat soaked through his clothes.

'Would you care for some tea?' Laura's clipped English tones outside the door shook his brain back into gear.

'No thanks, but I could do with a shower if that's okay?' Somehow he kept his voice steady.

'Of course. The hot water doesn't last long but it's okay if you don't dawdle. I'll fix us something on toast for supper when you're done.'

'Great.' He couldn't imagine what 'something on toast' might be but right now he didn't care as long as she left him alone. Hunter needed time to get control of himself before facing Laura's eagle-eyed scrutiny again.

★ ★ ★

Maybe she'd simply startled him from a nap but Hunter's sharp response hinted at more going on under his affable surface. She shouldn't be interested in knowing.

Before she half-drowned waiting for him at the bus station, Laura had planned on them eating dinner at the local pub but she wasn't venturing out again tonight. During her short-lived marriage she'd struggled to live up to Mike's expectations of coming home to a gourmet home-cooked meal every evening but now her usual go-to dinners arrived in the form of frozen calorie-counted meals, tinned soup or beans on toast. None of those would fill up Hunter McQueen's big toe.

Laura grabbed the Chinese restaurant menu off the fridge and made a quick phone call. Tonight the extra fee for delivery would be worth every penny.

'Almost human again.'

She told herself it was nothing more than ditching the travel-stained black clothes and replacing them with faded blue jeans and a crisp white shirt rolled up at the elbows that caught her eye.

The magic of a hot shower had turned Hunter's straggly dark ponytail into a curtain of black silk brushing his massive shoulders.

'You all right?'

'Perfectly well, thank you.' Laura cleared her throat. 'I hope you don't mind but I've ordered Chinese.'

'You eat it on toast here? Never tried that but I'm game for anything.'

'Don't be daft.' The pop of a wicked smile told her she'd fallen for his warped sense of humour again. 'I don't cook much these days and, on second thoughts, it struck me that you would probably consider beans on toast a starter rather than a main course.'

'You've got me intrigued.'

Laura's face burned. Men were never 'intrigued' by her.

'What sort of beans do you eat on toast anyway? Pinto? Navy? Lima?'

'Heinz.' She rifled in the cupboard and thrust a tin in his face. 'I've never heard of the others.'

'Your education's sorely lacking,

then.' His dramatic head shake made her laugh in spite of herself. 'But we've got time to remedy that.'

The doorbell saved her.

He guessed she wasn't an eating with chopsticks out of the boxes sort of woman and rummaged around the kitchen for a couple of plates and some cutlery. He should never have agreed to Polly's request. The English weather was as crappy as he remembered, he'd bet his life savings Johnny would be more shocked than pleased to see him and Ms Laura Williams disturbed him worse than a tornado in a wheat field.

'Really?' Swinging a bag in each hand she smiled the table. 'I thought single men ate straight from the takeaway box.'

'I reckon we both made assumptions.' Her eyes widened and he added another mistake to the list. *They're not a muddy-brown, idiot. Try creamy milk chocolate laced with rich golden cara-mel if you're gonna be accurate.*

'Let's eat while it's still hot.' The wobble in her voice disturbed Hunter. He wasn't vain but he also wasn't dumb. Her swift appraisal of his improved appearance sent up red warning flags. 'I ordered a selection. Egg rolls, tempura shrimp, sweet and sour pork, spicy Szechuan chicken, vegetable fried rice and my favourite Mongolian beef.'

'Perfect.'

'Beer?' She grabbed two bottles from a tiny fridge no bigger than the ones usually seen in American hotel rooms and passed one across the table to him.

'Thanks. I'm starved.'

'Didn't the coach make any stops so you could get something to eat?'

'Nope, only to pick up folk but I guess most knew that and they came prepared.' He didn't expand on his amusement at the foil wrapped sandwiches and thermos flasks produced by most of his fellow travellers. 'My seat mate forced a slice of his mom's fruit cake on me and it

18

wasn't bad. Damn sight better than the nasty ones we have at Christmas.' Helping himself to some of everything on offer he dug in. 'That hot chicken sure hits the spot.'

'Good.'

They ate in contented silence and soon they'd both finished.

'Help yourself to seconds.' Laura gestured towards the leftovers.

'No thanks. It'll do for breakfast.'

'Breakfast? I . . . '

'Gotcha.' Hunter chuckled. 'Isn't it supposed to be the single man go-to, along with cold pizza?'

'Very funny, I'm sure.' He watched her stiffen with annoyance. Their sense of humour obviously wasn't on the same wavelength. 'So tell me what your connection is with Johnny? Polly gave the impression you two were friends from when he lived in London growing up.'

'Yeah, we were in school together for a couple of years when my dad's company transferred him over here for a while.' The half-truth tripped out. Leaving his response there he faked a yawn and hoped she'd get the hint.

'Sorry. You must be dead on your feet.'

'Yep, I sure am. Seems to be catchin' up with me. I could promise I won't be as grouchy in the morning but you might not recognise the difference.'

'We'll see, won't we?'

'I'll help you clear up dinner first.'

'Leave it. I'm no domestic goddess but I can manage the leftovers and a few dishes.'

Hunter didn't press the point. He would honour his promise to Polly and then leave Laura to the peace she clearly preferred.

3

'I'm on my way over.' Polly giggled. 'I can't stay long because I've got a hair appointment but I'm dying to meet our hunky Yank.'

She should have expected her curious sister wouldn't be able to resist the temptation to check out her houseguest.

'For God's sake tell me you've got a pot of decent coffee brewing. I know y'all are a nation of tea drinkers but that won't hack it today.' Hunter sloped into the kitchen in the middle of tugging a thick grey jumper over his head. It only reached its final destination after giving Laura an eyeful of rock-hard stomach and a shadow of fine dark hair disappearing into the baggy sweatpants hanging low on his hips. She mentally begged for an Arctic breeze to settle around her neck like an invisibility cape.

'Is this your version of not as grouchy?'

'Before a heavy caffeine fix it's the best I can manage.' His eyes gleamed. 'I promise I'll soon be back to my normal sparkling self if I'm treated right.'

'Polly's stopping by here for a few minutes to meet you.' Did a trickle of anxiety sneak into his expression or was she reading too much into things as usual?

'Cool.'

'Here you go.' She filled her largest mug and passed it over. 'I'm not much of a cook but my coffee is legendary.'

'You're a lifesaver.'

'Cream and sugar?' His thick eyebrows shot up. 'Thought not.' She winced as he gulped down the scalding liquid. 'Do you have an asbestos mouth?'

'Did the famed British trait of unfailing politeness skip a generation with you?'

'Sorry.'

'I'm only teasing.' Hunter gave a lopsided grin. 'I guess I need to wave a sign over my head before I crack any jokes.'

'Breakfast?' She ignored his flippant remark. 'I can do toast or there's muesli in the cupboard?'

'Don't fret. I rarely eat before noon and if jet lag messes me around there's always the leftover Chinese.'

'How do you know I haven't polished it off myself?'

'Your horror last night gave you away.'

'Cooee, I'm here.' Her sister flung open the door and breezed in.

*   *   *

'You must be Johnny's beautiful bride.' Hunter jumped up and stuck out his hand, remembering Laura's aversion to the hug he dished out when they met. Clearly his old friend's taste in women hadn't changed. This woman fitted what he remembered of Johnny's preferences to a tee. A heart-shaped face with all the features in perfect proportion, clear blue eyes and tumbling blonde curls. They combined with a figure out of the perfect section of the human catalogue, if such a thing existed, to make one flat-out beautiful woman. Hunter caught Laura's wry smile. She must have watched many men skim over her and turn their attention on her younger sister over the years.

'Thanks, you're a flatterer but I'll take the compliment. If you aren't too tired I think Laura was planning to take you to Dartmoor this afternoon. Blow away the cobwebs from your journey.' Polly smiled. 'The weather isn't too awful and it'll give you a chance to sample a Devon cream tea as well.'

He supposed the light grey sky and soft drizzle were an improvement on the grim torrential rain when he arrived. 'Sounds great, but don't you need her to hang around and help with wedding stuff?'

'Good grief, no. Wedding arrangements aren't Laura's thing and anyway I've got everything under control. I do need you to share a few stories from Johnny's past so I can embarrass him when necessary but there isn't time now so think about it and I'll catch up with you later.'

Hunter nodded while wondering what stories he could safely use. 'It'd be my pleasure.'

'Bye, sis.' She left at the same breakneck speed with which she'd arrived.

★   ★   ★

Laura scraped a thin smear of butter on her toast. 'You didn't seem too disappointed when Polly rushed off. Are there stories about you and Johnny she would prefer not to hear?'

'It's all old news. Not worth digging up.'

She was adept at recognising a lie when she heard one these days and the faint tic in his right cheek gave Hunter away.

'I'm curious. What do you do for a living?'

Changing the subject was another giveaway. She could afford to play along for now. 'I'm the nursing ward manager of the A&E department at Derriford hospital just up the road from here.'

'I bet you run it like a well-oiled machine.'

'They call me the Enforcer.' Her admission made him smile. 'Let's get ready and leave before the weather changes.'

'Rainwear and hiking boots?'

'Yes if you've got them.' As a medical professional she rationalised her strong physical reaction to this man as nothing more than rampant pheromones but the emotional tug he exerted disturbed her far more.

'Feel free to bail on me. I won't tell Polly,' he said. 'If you don't mind giving me a key, we can both go off and do our own thing. I could be way off base but I'm picking up the sense you'd rather be on your own and that's fine with me.' An apology stuck in her throat but she couldn't explain her reserved attitude without talking about Mike, something she had no intention of doing. She retrieved a spare set of keys from the junk drawer and dropped them in his outstretched hand. If she still headed for Dartmoor she wouldn't be completely lying to Polly later, something she hated doing — although there were certain aspects of her ill-fated marriage her younger sister would be shocked to discover. Laura's role as protective older sister ran deep and she refused to spoil Polly's optimism about her upcoming wedding with her own deep-rooted cynicism. Johnny was a very different man from Mike, at least she fervently hoped so, but how well could anyone really know another person?

A few minutes later she heard Hunter slam the front door on his way out and hurried upstairs to throw on a warmer jumper before retrieving her neglected boots from the back of the wardrobe. On the way out she tugged on the only hat she could find in a hurry; an ugly red woolly one with wobbly reindeer ears that Polly had put in her Christmas stocking.

'Very cute. All you need is a red Rudolph nose and you'll be all set.' Hunter McQueen lounged against her car. 'I couldn't resist finding out what a cream tea is.' His mischievous smile re-emerged. 'Plus I figured we might as well make the best of being forced to spend these couple of days together. All the better to keep your sister happy.'

Laura resented having logic and common-sense used against her.

'Do we have a deal?' He stuck out his hand in a challenge and stared her down.

4

If she realised how alike they were, Laura would turn tail and flee. Hunter used his innately southern, talkative, tactile side to cover up the darker aspects of his personality while Laura retreated behind conventional British reserve. She carried a perpetual air of cautiousness about her, as though if she dared to relax for even a moment bad things would happen. The old expression about still waters running deep could have been written for them both.

'I thought we were tryin' to keep Polly happy?'

Laura reluctantly shook his hand. 'Fine.' The reluctant concession was obviously the best he'd get and Hunter grabbed her hand.

'Ouch. If you don't mind I'd prefer to have some bones left intact when you're done.'

Hunter chuckled and made a point of waggling each of her short, sturdy fingers. 'You're good.'

'I thought we were trying to be . . . cordial.'

'Cordial? Who on God's green earth uses that word outside of the boring English Lit classes they forced us to endure in high school?'

'Are you calling Charles Dickens and Jane Austen boring?'

'Just callin' it as I see it. No red-blooded American boy who spent his teenage years obsessing about football, girls and his first car cared a hoot for them.' He laid on the ignorant, male cliché with a trowel out of pure self-defence.

'I can only imagine.' Laura's mouth twitched and her cheeks puffed with the effort of not laughing. One day he'd catch her out and discover what a genuine smile would do to her everyday serious expression. He suspected the transformation would blindside him. 'Do you want to go to Dartmoor or not?' she asked him.

'The rain's gettin' worse.'

She examined the grey, sodden sky. 'Welcome to Devon in January. It's one of the most unpredictable months of the year and that's saying something.' Laura's piercing gaze swept him from head to toe. 'You've got a waterproof coat and decent boots. Unless American men are constructed in a vastly different way from British ones you won't melt in a touch of water.'

A touch of water? he thought to himself incredulously. 'I'm game if you are. At least I've got a resident nurse on hand if I catch pneumonia.' Hunter eased into the passenger seat and bumped his knees on the dash before tucking his legs out of the way. 'Your reindeer ears are drooping, Rudolph.'

★   ★   ★

Laura tossed the damp hat on the back seat and cringed at her reflection. Her unremarkable brown hair was squashed flat on the top before frizzing out

31

around the edges like an overcooked fried egg. She didn't wear the bed-head look well.

'I could mess mine up too if it'll make you feel better.'

Why couldn't she laugh along with him? *Because letting down your guard is dangerous.* Much better he took her for a humourless prig. 'Have you heard of Dartmoor?' She noticed Hunter's eyes shade to a dark unreadable shade of indigo.

'Vaguely, but give me the tourist spiel. I expect you've been practising.'

Laura ignored the gibe and rattled off all she knew about the national park on her doorstep. 'It takes its name from the River Dart that runs through it and it's extremely beautiful in a stark uncompromising way. That's probably why I love it. I'm not one for soft and pretty.' She threw him a half-smile. 'No argument? You're slacking.'

'I'm trying to be 'cordial'.'

Another driver cut her up and she barely slammed on her brakes in time to avoid ramming into the back of a flashy Mercedes.

'I guess we'd better stick to the tourist commentary. The weather's too bad for . . . sparring.'

She was certain he almost said flirting. 'If you're into ancient history there are Neolithic tombs, Bronze Age circles and abandoned medieval farmhouses. Anyone keen on geology heads towards the tors. They're big rock formations dotted all over the place and seriously impressive. My plan for the day included a hike, the visitor centre in Princetown and checking out the nearby prison. Most people have a morbid curiosity about the place because it was constructed during the Napoleonic Wars and is still in use.'

'I'm happy to give the prison a miss, but a hike would be good.'

Laura forced herself to be realistic. 'I know what I said about the rain but it is getting worse.'

'I sure love that British understatement.'

'I suggest we head straight for the

visitor centre then have lunch in one of the pubs. The weather might improve later.'

'I guess livin' here you've gotta be optimistic.'

'It helps.'

Hunter grinned. 'Remember to please Polly we've got to track down one of these cream tea things at some point.'

'Don't worry, the Wayside Cafe in Widdicombe will solve that problem later this afternoon.'

'I'm guessin' she's been extra good to you somewhere along the line to make you so keen to please her?'

Laura exhaled a heavy sigh. 'Are you always this persistent?'

'I've been called worse.'

'Why doesn't that surprise me?'

'No clue.'

'I'm going to concentrate on driving now while you admire the scenery.'

Hunter pressed his face against the window. 'Admiring the scenery. Happy?'

Laura's stubborn silence set off another of his deep, rumbling laughs.

Stark and uncompromising. The description suited the woman next to him as well as the bleak landscape. Perhaps on a bright sunny day both would soften.

Laura stopped the car in front of a large impressive building.

'Neat place.' He clambered out to join her on the pavement.

'Years ago this used to be a fancy hotel.' When she reached out to brush away a strand of wet hair clinging to his face her soft touch startled him. 'Your coat has a hood in case you hadn't noticed.'

'Why spoil the fun?'

'Because it's wiser.'

'You always do wiser?'

'No, but I usually wish I had.'

Hunter looped his arm through hers. 'Show me the wonders of the Princetown Visitor Centre and we'll consider our other options later.'

'Other?'

'Whether to eat lunch or head

straight for the tea and scones.'

A tiny smile played around her lips. 'It's a very important decision.'

Not half as big as the one spinning around his brain about whether to confess some distinctly un-wise things to this fascinating, aggravating woman.

5

For a brief respite from Hunter's disturbing presence she claimed she'd seen the main exhibition a million times and left him to wander around alone while she checked out the new display of work by local artists instead. The paintings didn't hold her attention and her thoughts drifted back to Polly's upcoming wedding. Last week she'd been stupid and attempted to point out what she saw as a few home truths.

We survived losing Mum and Dad because we stuck together and you were my rock when Mike destroyed my world. Can't you see that playing Russian roulette with a loaded gun is safer than walking down the aisle? Move in with Johnny if you must, but please don't tie yourself to him.

Polly had simply laughed in her face. *Oh Laura, we're choosing to be tied to each other because we don't want to make it easy to leave. We hope to start a family sooner rather than later, and I know you don't get that either. All you've ever wanted is to be a nurse and that's great for you but I'm different.*

Why hadn't she confessed the truth to Polly then? Would her sister have understood if she had explained that she loved her job but also longed to have a baby? Before she married Mike they agreed that they didn't want children right away. That was fair enough but later she discovered that he had interpreted it as meaning she didn't want them at all. His outright refusal to even consider the possibility hurt Laura more than his serial infidelity. Now she saw that spoke volumes about their doomed marriage.

'Hey, are you all right?'

She jerked away as Hunter touched her arm and rushed from the room. Barely able to see through her tears she only stopped when he caught up with her outside.

'I'm sorry. I didn't mean — '

' — I know. It's me.' Laura swiped at the rain trickling down her face. 'Oh damn this weather.'

With a flourish he pulled her reindeer hat from his pocket, tugged it over her head and tucked a stray curl in out of the way. 'I guessed this might come in handy. A droopy reindeer is better than nothing.'

'If you say so.' Despite her best efforts, his gentle humour drew her in and she managed a wan smile. 'Let's make a dash for the pub before we're washed away.'

'They won't mind us dripping all over the place?'

'Don't be daft.' Laura pushed open the old wood door. 'If the Plume of Feathers disliked damp customers they'd have gone bankrupt donkey's years ago. They've been serving wet, muddy hikers since the eighteenth century so our fairly respectable sogginess won't bother them in the slightest. Mind your head, though; the ceilings are low.'

'I'm always scanning the landscape for potential hazards.' Hunter winked.

'Including Englishwomen with dangerous smiles.'

There was no way to respond without stepping into a potential minefield.

He gazed around with an approving nod. 'This ticks every cliché about English pubs. Old wood beams. Slate floor. Antique furniture. Hunting prints on the walls.' Hunter gestured towards the huge brick fireplace flanked by a basket of wood and a set of gleaming brass fire tools. 'I'm gonna stake my spot.' He stood with his back to the blazing logs. 'I wouldn't mind samplin' one of the locally brewed ales.'

'They've several from the Dartmoor Brewery up the road. 'I'll get our drinks and bring back a menu.'

'Thanks. I'll have a pint of whatever the barman recommends.'

While she waited to be served Laura caught Hunter's deep voice rumbling in the background and glanced back over her shoulder to see him deep in conversation with a couple of local farmers. There was something chameleon-like about the man, as though he became whatever was necessary to fit in. Warning bells jangled in her head.

★   ★   ★

'There's a Jail Ale for you and a soda water and lime for the poor driver.'

He wasn't sure what he'd done to rattle her again but her humorous words weren't reflected in her cool expression. Hunter sniffed the deep brown, hoppy brew before taking a long satisfying swallow. 'Boy, that's good.'

'Better than that weak Yankee stuff that's not fit to be called beer?' one of the local men yelled over, and when Hunter told him where to stick his head, including the words 'sun' and 'not shining', it elicited a rough laugh from his new acquaintances.

'We'd better sit down before you start a riot.'

'Pick a table.'

'This'll do.' Laura flopped down in the nearest chair and thrust a menu at him.

'Put me out of my misery and tell me what the heck a Cumberland ring is? I assume y'all don't eat jewellery.'

'It's a meaty sausage flavoured with herbs and shaped into a ring.'

'That's a relief.' A tiny smile eked out of her flattened lips. 'I'm gonna give the mixed grill a try.' With enough meat to horrify a vegetarian and the word 'fried' repeated multiple times, he suspected he might not have to eat again until tomorrow. 'What's tempting you?' He leaned forward inches away from Laura's face. 'After last night, don't claim you're a salad in all weathers girl. That Mongolian beef didn't stand a chance.'

'I'll ignore your rudeness.'

'That was supposed to be a joke.' Hunter sighed. 'Tell me what you want and I'll order. I'm starved.'

'Oh, get me the chilli con carne.' Laura was clearly exasperated but too fed up to argue. Hunter wasn't sure if that counted as a win on his part but hurried off to the bar before she could nix his small triumph.

6

For two pins she'd walk out and leave him stranded, but no doubt he'd secure a ride back to Plymouth with one of his new friends. Everyone took to him except for her . . . or at least that's what she was telling herself.

'I'm surprised you're still here. I thought you'd do a runner while my back was turned.' Hunter sunk into his chair, stuck his long legs out towards the fire and rested his large hands behind his head. 'Thought about it, didn't you?' Laura's grim silence seemed to amuse him. 'It was considerate of you to let me warm up some more. We might even be dry when it's time to leave.' He tugged the rubber band from his ponytail and shook out the damp, heavy mass of hair. A few stray raindrops glistened on the inky surface. 'Are you off work until after the weekend?'

43

'Um, yes. Why?'

'Give me a break, Laura. It's not a trick question.'

'Sorry.' She picked at a hangnail. 'I go back on Monday and then I'm off again on Friday until after the wedding. What about you?'

'My plans are . . . fluid.'

'I assume you've got a return flight booked?'

'Can't wait to get rid of me?'

'One mixed grill and one chilli.' The young waitress set down their plates.

'Thanks, honey.'

'You're American.' The girl's voice rose along with the colour in her cheeks.

Before she could chip in with a sarcastic response, Laura's jaw dropped as the very man they were supposed to avoid strolled into the pub. Johnny had his arm draped around a stunning brunette who definitely wasn't Polly. 'Shush.' Her panic must have shown because for once he obeyed without asking a million and one questions. 'Don't turn around.'

'What's wrong?' The waitress frowned.

44

'Ketchup.' Hunter whispered. 'We need ketchup.'

By her puzzled expression the girl had them marked down as a pair of lunatics. Any second now things would get worse.

* * *

'Hunter? Hunter McQueen?' A familiar British accent rang out. 'What the bloody hell are you doing here?'

He watched his old friend turn ashen. Johnny Matthews wasn't the skinny, pimple-faced boy Hunter remembered but there was no mistaking him. That was not the face of a pleasantly surprised man.

'Laura?' Johnny gawked at them both now and beads of sweat popped out on his forehead. 'Oh God. Polly's not here, is she?'

'No. Aren't you the lucky one? I suppose you assumed you were safe coming this far away from Plymouth?'

'What do you mean?'

'Does your 'friend' know you're

45

getting married on Saturday?'

'Oh, Laura don't be daft.' A trace of Johnny's familiar roguish smile appeared. 'This is Emily Stephens. You must've heard Polly talk about her Irish friend Em? They were roommates when she worked in Dublin for a while after uni.'

Hunter shouldn't find it quite so amusing to see Laura struck dumb.

'I wanted to surprise Polly with something more original than a male stripper at the party.'

'She'll be thrilled.' Laura smiled at the other woman.

'I'm Hunter McQueen by the way.' He introduced himself to the attractive Irishwoman. 'I'm the other party surprise, at least I was supposed to be, and no I'm not a male stripper.'

'Pity.' The frank appraisal made him laugh.

'This is a bloody mess.' Laura groused.

'Yeah it sure is. Our food is getting cold.'

'Our food?'

'Why don't you let them get their

drinks while we start to eat and they can come back to join us when they're ready?' Hunter suggested.

'Great idea.' Johnny steered Emily towards the bar.

'At least you're a hit with one lady.'

'Should I apologise for that too?'

Laura gave him a silent, sideways glance. 'No.'

Hunter dragged a French fry through the pile of ketchup. 'Eat.' The gruff order should have earned him another sharp response but for some reason she did as he asked.

'Am I right to think Polly made a mistake inviting you? Johnny didn't seem very thrilled.'

'Yeah, she sure did. But I made a bigger one in accepting.'

'Will you explain it all to me later?'

He spotted Johnny and Emily heading their way. 'Sure.'

Hunter raised his glass. 'Let's drink to you and your lovely bride.'

'I don't have a clue what she sees in me.' Johnny laughed and shook his

47

head. 'I'm snatching her up before she realizes I'm a plonker. I bet you don't even know what one of those is?'

'It's the English version of an Irish eejit.' Em tossed Hunter a provocative smile. 'I'd be happy to teach you a few colloquialisms, Mr McQueen.'

I bet you would, thought Hunter.

'What are you doing here anyway, McQueen?' Johnny probed.

'*You* kept regaling my dear sister with stories about your long lost best friend,' Laura chipped in. 'Of course sweet, kind-hearted Polly thought you'd be thrilled to see Hunter again.'

'What about me?' Emily frowned, obviously unsure about her own welcome.

'Oh, you'll be a brilliant surprise,' Johnny assured her.

'I think it's time we were going.'

He jumped on Laura's suggestion. 'Sure is. We'll see you both at the party on Saturday.' Hunter sprang up, tossed his coat over his arm and whisked her out of the pub. 'The weather's still crappy. Let's skip the tea shop for today and head back to your beige palace.'

'My house?'

'Sorry, beige palace was a tad cruel,' he conceded. 'I'm takin' a wild guess it's question answerin' time.' Depending how honest he decided to be, Hunter might find himself kicked out on the street.

7

Beige palace? The man had a nerve. According to her estate agent magnolia was the perfect neutral colour for increasing the resale value. Laura massaged shampoo into her scalp until it tingled and gave her hair a quick rinse. She ought to spend the money and buy an electric shower or replace her immersion heater with one that lasted more than a meagre five minutes before tailing off to cold.

Had a good day with the hunk?

She hadn't replied to Polly's teasing text yet. They were about as close as sisters could be despite their differences, or *maybe* because of them. Laura was career-focused, undomesticated and had little tolerance for weakness. Soft-hearted Polly taught in a nursery school and could be a spokesperson for the latest Danish hygge craze with her romantic nature, unwavering belief in the innate goodness of people and deep love of home comforts.

'Are you nearly done in there?' Hunter's gravelly drawl dragged her back to reality.

'I won't be long.' She tugged on an old black fleece top and grey joggers, completing the seductive outfit with another of Polly's Christmas gifts: fluffy red socks with flapping red reindeer noses to match her much maligned hat. 'There you go it's all yours.' A whoosh of heat zoomed up her face as Hunter strolled across the narrow hall, shirtless and swinging a towel in his hand.

'All right if I go in now or are you good to ogle a bit longer?'

If his grin spread any wider he could double for the Cheshire Cat. 'Could you possibly be any vainer?' Laura stiffened and stepped away. She had made a terrible fool of herself over one man and didn't plan on repeating the experience.

★　★　★

He hadn't stirred her up on purpose but whatever flicker of attraction lingered between them needed to be nipped in the bud anyway, so this worked. 'I'll go and have that shower before I catch pneumonia. Why don't you put the kettle on? Doesn't that usually work miracles?' Laura's raised eyebrows said that wouldn't do the trick this time. 'See you downstairs.'

Why did she make him so reckless? He put it down to the drift of warm roses surrounding her, the soft golden brown hair framing her face and the way her gaze travelled over him while the tip of her pink tongue traced the outline of her generous mouth.

Long, cold shower time.

Hunter didn't hurry to get dressed, and when he reached the kitchen door Laura's raised voice stopped him in his tracks. When everything went quiet he dared to tap on the door.

'It's safe to come in. I won't bite your head off.'

'Did someone rile you up?'

'You could say that.'

'Want to talk about it?'

'No.' Laura snapped. 'You'll have to make do with instant coffee. I can't be bothered to wait around.' She sloshed boiling water into two mugs and gave them a vicious stir.

'I'll drink tea if it's easier and I could take mine upstairs and leave you to it.'

Laura waved around her mobile phone. 'That was my boss. He's stressed out because there's a nasty stomach bug doing the rounds, which means more patients and an equivalent staff shortage. He begged me to cut short my holiday but if I agree Polly will have my guts for garters.'

Her bizarre turn of phrase made him smile.

'It's not funny.'

'Yeah, it is. Guts for garters?'

'I've always heard that expression.' She gave him a quizzical look. 'I'm sure you've got a few strange ones too.'

'We sure do. The south is famous for them. Of course they've got to be said with the right accent or they sound dumb.'

'And they don't sound dumb with it?'

Hunter wagged his finger. 'Did no one tell you you're supposed to be polite to guests and not mock the way they talk?' Two pink circles blossomed on her cheeks. 'I'm jokin'' He took a sip of the insipid, coffee-flavoured liquid and almost spat it out. 'I'm not a baby. Go to work. Polly won't hear it from me.'

'She'll find out.' Laura grumbled. 'For a sweet person she's incredibly cunning.' Her face darkened. 'She'll find out about you and Johnny too. Whatever the pair of you are hiding, she'll worm the truth from him.'

Hunter pulled out his phone. 'What's Polly's number?'

'Why?'

'Because I'm gonna call her.'

'You can't!'

'Watch me.'

'You are one stubborn man.'

Slathering on his southern charm with a trowel he spun a touching story of how desperate the hospital was for Laura's skills until he had Polly eating out of his hand. 'Grovel.' Hunter whispered and passed over the phone.

After a quick chat she handed it back. 'I've promised I'll be through working by Saturday lunchtime.'

'Fair enough.'

Laura swallowed a mouthful of coffee, winced and threw the rest down the sink. 'That's vile.' Before he could stop her she snatched his mug and treated it the same way. 'You didn't fly four thousand miles to be poisoned by cheap, supermarket coffee.'

'Off you go and do your Florence Nightingale bit. Did I mention I've got a thing about nurses?'

'For heaven's sake.' She shook her head. 'The days of starched white aprons and black stockings are long gone.'

'Yeah I know. Pity.' Hunter exhaled an exaggerated sigh. 'You're gonna kill me, Nurse Williams.'

'Senior Charge Nurse if you don't mind, Mr McQueen.'

Laura's wobbly voice threw up another set of red warning flags. 'Off with you.'

'Thanks,' she whispered. 'You're a . . .'

'A what?'

'Nothing. It doesn't matter.'

There were several ways he'd prefer she finished the sentence, but Laura hurried out of the kitchen and left it to his imagination.

8

'There you go, strong and black like me.' Henry flashed his toothy grin around the staff room door and held out a steaming paper cup.

Laura's weary laughter deepened his smile. 'Why are you so bloody cheerful? I doubt you slept more than four hours in the last twenty-four and today won't be much better.'

He set the cup on the table, dropped to one knee and grabbed her right hand. 'When are you going to put me out of my misery and marry me?'

They enacted this ritual at six-monthly intervals and if she ever said yes Henry would die of a heart attack on the spot. For ten years they'd worked together and were closer than many real-life couples but without the complication of loving each other 'that' way. He understood that her uncharacteristic flare of anger on the phone earlier arose from frustration. Like him she saw the A&E department as her second family and carried an overwhelming loyalty towards their patients.

'Being Polly's bridesmaid next week is the closest I plan on getting to an altar again.' He understood her reasons more than anyone else. In the rare quiet patches when they both worked night shifts she'd confided things to him that she'd never shared with her sister. Henry tried to warn her off Mike when she first started dating the handsome surgeon but kept his counsel once they got engaged. Later on he spent hours listening patiently as she described her husband's increasingly domineering behaviour, followed by Mike's complete about turn when he lost all interest in her and began a string of blatant affairs.

'Remember — '

' — never say never,' she parroted. 'Coming from Derriford Hospital's most confirmed bachelor that's hypocritical.'

'Time to get back to the trenches.'

Henry levered himself out of the faded, red plastic chair as the door opened.

'Excuse me.' A young nursing assistant poked her head in and motioned to Laura. 'There's a man downstairs looking for you.'

'Aren't you the lucky one?' Henry quipped.

'Does this man have a name?'

The girl blushed. 'He didn't give one, but he's American and really . . . '

' . . . big?'

'Uh yes.'

'We'll walk down together.' Henry's grin made Laura's heart sink. For a senior doctor he loved nothing better than juicy gossip and Hunter's appearance would make his day. She'd never hear the end of this.

'Thank you. I'll come right away.'

He fell into step with her and bided his time until they reached the empty lift.

'You might as well tell me about your mystery man now.'

Laura cobbled together a reasonable

explanation and was sure she'd got away with it until Henry poked her in the ribs as the lift door opened.

'Friends with benefits, eh?'

'Certainly not. I only met him on Wednesday . . .' The words dried in her throat.

Hunter, back to wearing his worn black jeans, denim jacket and cowboy boots flashed his trademark off-kilter smile. In one hand he wielded a large paper cup from the nearest coffee shop and in the other a white paper bag that wafted out the delicious aroma of fried bacon. Laura's stomach rumbled. She hadn't eaten since yesterday unless a couple of soggy digestives and a dried up satsuma counted. The receptionist stopped working to eye up Hunter, as did the man mopping the floor. Several patients waiting in the crowded seating area also switched their attention from the TV chat show on in the background.

'Mr McQueen, would you care to come into my office?' She threw Henry a sweet smile. 'I'll see you later, Doctor

Clarke.' Laura pointed out a dirty mark on the tiles to the cleaner before glancing around the busy room. That sent a message to the receptionist there were more important things to be done than mining Laura's personal life for interesting titbits of news to spread around the hospital. 'This way, Mr McQueen.'

★   ★   ★

Interesting. She'd been laughing with the smiling doctor when the lift doors opened, although Hunter didn't pick up on any sexual charge between them. The moment she stepped into the emergency department everything about her demeanour changed and he understood how she came by her nickname. The fact she wasn't wearing an old-fashioned starched uniform meant nothing. Her dark blue tunic and trousers, polished black shoes and neatly tied-back hair all remained immaculate despite the fact she'd been working for nearly ten hours already.

When he struggled awake this morning he got to thinking that the last
proper food she ate was probably at the
pub in Princetown because she only
had time to snatch a sandwich before
setting off to work last night. Deciding
to bring her breakfast was a spur of the
moment decision and it never occurred
to him that he'd stir up unwelcome
gossip. Back in Nashville he didn't stand
out, but here he might as well brandish
a neon sign announcing the arrival of a
big, brash American chasing after one
of their nurses. He noticed that she
didn't close the office door and suspected that was done on purpose, like
most of Laura's actions. She wouldn't
want anyone to jump to conclusions
about their relationship.

'What are you doing here?'

'Bringing you breakfast.' Hunter waved
the coffee under her nose and grinned
when she snatched it from his hand. He
manoeuvred a massive bacon sandwich
out of the bag. 'You must be starving. I
made this with my own fair hands.'

62

'I thought only Disney princesses have fair hands, but I won't argue.'

'That'll be a first.'

She grabbed the sandwich and took a quick bite. 'I should be working.'

'You need to refuel.'

'What's your plan for the day? I'll be heading home by mid-morning and crashing. I've got the night shift again.'

'I might wander into Plymouth and take a look at the Mayflower Steps. I could fix us dinner later before you come back.'

'There's no need. If I get here early enough I'll buy something from the hospital café.' Laura lowered her voice. 'I'll intend to pick up a healthy salad but smell the pasties cooking and won't be able to resist. That's the usual way of it, I'm afraid.'

'From my point of view it's not doin' you any harm.'

'And of course you're never wrong.'

The things he didn't say lingered between them. 'I'll leave you to wallow in all the blood and gore.'

'Are you squeamish?'

'A complete wuss,' he admitted. 'I screw up my eyes in horror movies. I don't care that it's fake. My older brother used to watch and tell me when it was safe to look again.'

'Ms Williams, are we likely to have the pleasure of your company anytime soon? One of my patients arrived without the relevant X-rays and I need you to track them down immediately. I was coming this way so I thought I'd save my nurse the trouble. I don't like to consider myself above the fray.'

Laura sprang away as if she'd been stung. A heavy-set man in a starched white coat glared at them from the doorway and his intrusive pale grey eyes sent a shiver down Hunter's spine.

'My apologies, I didn't realise you were with a patient.'

Hunter thought the man couldn't sound less apologetic if he'd tried. 'I'm not. Not guilty of being a patient that is.' The doctor's stony expression didn't alter. 'Hunter McQueen from Nashville,

Tennessee. I'm simply a friend bringin' sustenance to a poor starving nurse.'

'Really.' The man's thin lips curled in a dismissive sneer. 'Senior Charge Nurse Williams the phrase 'private life' means you conduct it outside of this hospital. Do I make myself clear?'

'You're hardly one to . . . ' Laura bit her lip. 'Of course, *sir*.' The man's face tightened at her unmistakeable disdain. Hunter waited for him to rip into her but he spun around and strode off, the heels of his glossy black wingtips clicking on the tiles.

'I must go back to work.' A hint of pleading laced through her words, begging him not to ask any questions.

'Yeah, sorry I caused a stir.'

The faintest tinge of amusement pulled at her mouth. 'I suspect that's your mission in life. Now shoo.' She swiftly brushed by him and sped past the gaggle of people hanging around near the waiting room. Hunter couldn't help noticing he attracted more than a few glances and whisperings as he left by a side door.

Outside he hiked up his collar against the heavy drizzle darkening the sky but before he could pull out his phone to call for a taxi a balled up fist slammed into his stomach. Through the excruciating pain he focused long enough to recognise the arrogant doctor who crossed swords with Laura.

'Go home where you belong, Yank.'

He groaned and his world dissolved into a terrifying blackness.

9

'Uh, nurse, I hate to bother you but I'm a bit worried. There's a man outside lying on the ground. I can't tell if he's asleep or drunk.'

Laura almost told the elderly woman they didn't have time to check on every homeless person who loitered around the warm hospital but remembered Florence Nightingale. The icon to nurses around the world put her success down to never either making or taking any excuses. Being rattled by her ex-husband's boorish manner didn't excuse Laura's lack of compassion.

'Thank you. I'll send someone to check on him.' The woman's cherry-red coat rang a bell. 'How is your husband doing?' She recalled they'd recently admitted him after a heart attack.

'Jim's coming home tomorrow.'

'That's wonderful news. It was kind

67

of you to trouble yourself about the man outside.'

'It's no trouble, dearie.' The woman's pale blue eyes swam with tears. 'I only hope somebody will do the same for our boy Sam if he needs help, wherever he is.'

Laura didn't probe and nothing more was said. People had their pride. She beckoned Pete Richards over and he bounded across the waiting room like an exuberant puppy. The young man was straight out of training and would make a fine nurse when he learned to channel his energy. Laura returned to her paperwork in the hope that filling in routine forms would settle her down after the unexpected clash with Mike. On the rare occasions they bumped into each other they struggled to be polite, so why did he lay into her today? Polly would claim he was jealous but that was ridiculous. That particular unpleasant side of his personality faded where she was concerned once he found other more amenable women to practise his dubious charms on.

'I think you'd better come.' Pete's usual smile was now a worried frown. 'Someone told me earlier about your American . . . friend and, from the description, I think it might be him. He was unconscious when I arrived but he's come around now. Do you want me to call for a couple of porters and a stretcher?'

'Yes, do that while I go outside.' Her heart missed a beat at the sight of Hunter splayed out on the concrete with his head butting up against the brick wall. A grey pallor dulled his winter tan and his eyelids fluttered when she crouched next to him. 'Hunter, can you hear me?' He struggled to shift around but she placed a restraining hand on his shoulder. 'Don't move. We'll get you inside and evaluate you there.'

'I — '

' — We'll talk later.' Laura smoothed the hair away from his face. 'Please try to be still.'

'Where do you want him?' Foxy, the senior porter who'd worked at Derriford forever, appeared with one of his assistants.

'Cubicle four should be free.' Laura sprang back up. 'He's got a possible head injury.' She must remain professional at all costs. Her job involved clinical coordination, managing patient care and maintaining the quality of service and care in the accident and emergency department — not devoting all her attention to one favoured patient. Back inside she tracked down Pam. 'Would you mind taking over in four please and let me know when the doctor's evaluated the patient?' Putting her most trusted staff nurse in charge of Hunter was the best she could do. No doubt there was already a buzz bouncing around after her set-to with Mike. She'd seen, and deliberately ignored, several staff members who were hanging around outside her office when she came out but they must have overheard everything. This new incident would raise her several notches higher on the hospital gossip ladder.

Retreating to her office she returned to her neglected paperwork and dealt with multiple interruptions while keeping one eye on the clock. Exhaustion nibbled at the edges of her concentration and she found herself counting the minutes until it was time for the shift change.

'Sorry to bother you.' Pam stuck her head around the door. 'Mr McQueen's conscious but not up to talking and we need some information.' She appeared slightly uncomfortable. 'Nurse Richards said he's a personal friend of yours and thought you might be able to help.'

'Of course.' She raised her voice enough to carry through the half-open door. 'He's actually an old friend of my sister's fiancé and simply staying with me until the pre-wedding party tomorrow night. I only met him a couple of days ago and know very little about him.' That wasn't a complete lie because she had no clue what the man even did for a living.

The phrase 'private life' means you conduct it outside of this hospital.

Mike was within his rights to reprimand her earlier even if his attitude needed work. He was a perfect example of the theory that surgeons didn't need a good bedside manner because their patients were generally asleep.

No one else would have cause to question her behaviour today.

★   ★   ★

Through the avalanche of hammers beating against his skull Hunter struggled to focus on what Laura was saying. A few phrases drifted in and out of his hearing about a possible concussion and the need for next of kin details.

'Are you in pain, Mr McQueen?'

'Nah, I'm good.'

'We can give you something stronger — '

' — No!' His attempt to shout worsened his headache. He would grit his teeth and put up with any amount of pain rather than go down that particular rabbit hole again. His teenage years were strewn with bad decisions and stealing his mother's prescription painkillers on a regular basis to numb the emotions he couldn't handle ranked high up there on the list.

'We won't administer any drugs without your permission unless it's medically necessary and you aren't able to give consent.' Laura's firm, quiet voice soothed him. 'I promise. We'll send you up for a CT scan soon and, depending on the results, we may keep you tonight for observation.'

He almost cracked a joke about being happy for her to observe him anytime she liked, but he'd caused her enough embarrassment already. Before she came in he'd pretended to be worse than he really was when the examining doctor asked pertinent questions about what happened to him.

Would you recognise the person who hit you again? Do you want to report it to the police?

For Laura's sake he kept his mouth shut.

'I've written myself down as your point of contact for now, unless you prefer to use your family in America?'

'No. There's . . . no one close. You don't mind?' For a fleeting second her gaze softened and the woman behind the carefully maintained nurse's mask popped out. He hated lying to her but the truth would stir up more questions.

'Not at all. I'm sorry but I must return to my other patients. I'll check on you again later.'

Hunter gave himself up to the ministrations of a vigorous male nurse determined to practise his blood-drawing skills.

★ ★ ★

She enjoyed puzzles. From complicated jigsaws to mystery novels and cryptic crosswords, they all intrigued her and Hunter was her newest challenge.

There's no one close.

She doubted that very much but for whatever reason he didn't want to discuss his family.

'It's pants out there.' Daisy Mullins burst into the office, tugging down the hood of her fluorescent pink raincoat and shaking out a mass of frizzy black hair. 'It's been tipping down all night.' She hitched her coat over the back of a chair where it began to drip on the floor. 'Please tell me it's quiet in the madhouse today.'

'Hangover?'

'Moi? Never.' Her throaty laugh filled the room. 'Some of us have a social life. Sorry about that.'

In many ways they were on the same page because both women were childless divorcees who professionally had no patience with inefficiency or laziness. There the similarities ended, because Daisy regarded her own disastrous marriage as nothing more than a blip on the radar of life. Party invitations, blind dates and Tinder — she happily tried them all. Daisy was convinced that her true love was out there somewhere and her mission in life was to find him. Laura's lack of interest in throwing herself back in the dating pool bewildered her, and they'd had many late-night discussions on the subject. Laura stuck to the mantra that she was content with her single life.

Compared to being stuck in her miserable marriage she *was* content. Outside of work she answered to no one. That was an incredible lightening of the burden Mike had laid on her so stealthily it took her a while to recognise the difference between protective and possessive. Her quiet well-ordered exist-ence might not be how she had envisaged her life playing out, but she knew how much worse things could be. She wasn't chasing after another man to satisfy her longing for a child.

'Don't be sorry. I'm pleased one of us does.'

'I hear your Florence Nightingale halo got tarnished today.'

'Who told you?' Laura probed.

'News gets around.'

Daisy had been off work for the last three days but her web of informants rivalled the old KBG.

'Your ex is a prick.'

'He had a point.'

'Maybe, but he didn't have to throw his weight around. He's bloody rude and a bully.' Daisy's dimples blossomed and a wicked sparkle crept into her dark eyes. 'Are you going to confess every detail about your yummy American before I'm forced to drag it out of you?'

'Let's get the changeover out of the way first. I'm about dead on my feet.' She grabbed a handful of files from her desk.

Pam Mitchell hurried in. 'Sorry to interrupt but you asked me to keep you updated. Mr McQueen's been admitted to Tamar ward. We're keeping him twenty-four hours for observation because the MRI revealed this isn't his first concussion.'

'Thanks, Pam. When we're done here I'll make sure there's nothing he needs before I go home.'

She ignored the other two nurses' blatant smirks and launched into the standard routine for handing over care of the department. Pam got the hint and disappeared but not before giving Daisy a thumbs up sign.

Maybe she should make a belated New Year's Resolution to stick Hunter McQueen on the next plane back to Nashville.

10

'What's it supposed to be?' Hunter poked at the greyish blob on his plate running into a white puddle and surrounded by a pile of limp, pale green leaves.

'Mince, mashed potatoes and cabbage.'

He didn't bother to ask the fresh-faced young nurse what had been minced because he had no intention of risking his life eating it. Hospital food in the States didn't have a great reputation but was gourmet compared to this sludge. As the nurse disappeared to brighten the day of the patient next to him a familiar voice broke into his thoughts.

'Being troublesome, are we?' Laura appeared at the foot of his bed.

'Uh, no. Simply asking what's on the menu today.' He forced on a smile and shovelled a large forkful in his mouth.

'Is there anything you need me to bring in?'

Ear plugs to cover the inevitable snoring he'd suffer tonight from his five fellow internees, all elderly men? Pyjamas to cover up more than the standard issue skimpy gown? A juicy quarter pounder with cheese from the nearest fast food joint? On the plus side the ward was a generous size and hospitals kept lights on day and night so he wouldn't make a fool of himself by freaking out. 'Nah, I'm good.'

'Thank you for lying.' A sliver of amusement lightened her tired face.

'You're welcome.'

'But seriously, how are you doing?'

'I've been worse.'

Laura frowned. 'I'm not surprised. I saw your charts.'

To play for time, he crammed in another mouthful of lukewarm sludge.

'You've had other concussions.'

★ ★ ★

80

'I played football in high school. I'm talkin' about real football not your namby-pamby game. It was par for the course then. If you didn't get hurt you weren't playin' hard enough. The coach would check us out and if you could focus okay and didn't feel dizzy he stuck you back on the field.'

'That's appalling.'

'Yeah, well, they weren't as aware of the possible long-term effects I guess.'

'You need to be aware of any memory problems, trouble concentrating, personality changes and sudden sensitivity to light and noise.' Laura sounded stern. 'There are other symptoms too. I recommend regular check-ups because the sooner your doctor finds out something is wrong the more treatment options they have.'

'Yes ma'am.' Hunter closed his eyes and rested his aching head back on the pillow. Time to use the worn out patient card in case she started questioning him about his family again.

'Sorry, you must be exhausted. I'm

always telling hospital visitors to be considerate and I should take my own recommendations.' Her cool fingers stroked his dry skin and Hunter felt like the lowest form of pond life. 'They'll ring me if your condition changes, otherwise I'll be back in tonight around seven.' Laura's smile deepened. 'If it's any consolation none of the staff touches the mystery mince either.'

'I don't mean to be . . . '

'. . . obtuse? Awkward? Secretive?'

'The truth isn't overly exciting.'

'It often isn't, but we still avoid telling it because we're stubborn creatures.' Laura fixed him with her gimlet stare. 'Have you managed to recall any details yet of who did this to you?'

'Nope.'

'You're an appalling liar. I can't imagine why you won't say.'

With a silent shrug he closed his eyes again and willed her to leave. He didn't have the strength to lie again.

★ ★ ★

Laura couldn't decide why his lie bothered her so much because this time next week Hunter's brief foray into her life would be history. *Really?* She strode out of the ward without a backward glance and on the way to the car her mobile rang.

'What's the silly bugger done now?' Johnny asked.

'What particular silly bugger are we talking about?' As if she didn't know.

'Pete Richards told me Hunter is taking up one of our scarce hospital beds.'

Trust the chatty young nurse's reach to spread as far as the hospital's finance department, Johnny's domain. 'Someone jumped him outside A&E and we're keeping him overnight because he's got a concussion.'

'So he won't be well enough to 'surprise' me at the party tomorrow?' Johnny scoffed. 'Typical.'

'I'll break the news to Polly because you're not supposed to know he's here.'

'Is he well enough for visitors?'

'Not if you're going to upset him.'

'I wouldn't!'

'I mean it. They might let you pop in for a few minutes but if you cause any trouble, Senior Charge Nurse Painter will throw you out on your ear.'

'He's on Dracula's ward?'

'Yes.' Leo Painter's reputation was legendary. 'I'm off home now before I drop, and I'll ring Polly when I get there. I'll see you at the Acropolis tomorrow.'

Half an hour later she'd changed into her old, blue flannel pyjamas and made a steaming mug of tea loaded with sugar. Before she had time to ring Polly her sister burst into the house in a whirlwind of white-hot anger and tears.

'How could he not tell me something that important? He's supposed to love me.'

★ ★ ★

Hunter studied the stream of visitors coming in and out before spying the ideal person for his mission. He couldn't easily get the man's attention at the nurses' station because he'd been forbidden to leave his bed under threat of death. A slight exaggeration but the intimidating Leo Painter was only a few centimetres shorter than Hunter and weighed considerably more meaning he wasn't about to take the chance.

He turned his most engaging smile on the grey-haired woman cleaning the floor. 'Uh, nurse.'

'I'm not a nurse, lovie. Ring your bell if you need something.'

'I'm wonderin' if you could do me a favour.'

'Ooh, you're the American. Someone said we had one here. My man's a big John Wayne fan and you look ever so much like him.'

Her husband or John Wayne? he wondered.

'What it is you need, dear?'

He pointed towards the gangling young man who was the first person he remembered seeing when he regained consciousness. 'Could you ask that nurse to come and see me? I wanted to thank him for helping me when I had my . . . accident.'

'Of course, dearie.' She shuffled off to tackle his quarry. Hunter observed the man's initial confusion but his face cleared as the woman gestured at him.

'Hello, Mr McQueen. You're looking better.'

'I'm feeling it. Thanks to you. It is Pete, right?' He waffled on for a couple of minutes before mentioning Laura. No doubt this guy knew they were personally connected but he still inched his way around to the question he really wanted to ask. 'Who was that asshole doctor who was rude to her this morning? Someone should do us all a favour and re-arrange his face.'

'Join the queue.' Pete grimaced. 'No one can stand him. Believe it or not he's Nurse Williams' ex.'

'As in ex-husband?'

'Yes. Mr Mike Russell himself.'

'Mr? Why's he waltzing around in a white coat if he's not a doctor?'

Pete grinned. 'It's a weird British thing. He's a heart surgeon but when doctors become consultants we call them Mister. Bloody stupid if you ask me when they've trained for years and worked crippling hours.'

'So he's — '

' — a wanker,' Pete finished.

'Nurse Richards, I hope you have a good reason for disturbing my patient?'

Before Hunter could shoulder the blame he received a quelling glare.

'I'm sure you've got better things to do.' Painter's thick, black slug-like brows furrowed together. 'If you're still on my ward in ten seconds I'll put you on report.'

Smoke practically flew from Pete's heels as he race-walked out. Hunter guessed running was another of Leo Painter's no-no's.

'One word of warning, Mr McQueen. Certain senior members of staff resemble an octopus in the sense of having a long reach.' Painter glowered. 'Do I make myself clear?'

'You sure do.'

'Good.' He smoothed the covers on Hunter's bed and re-tucked the corners. No doubt some hapless junior would be treated to a refresher course in bed making later. 'The tea trolley will be around in a few minutes. After that I suggest you rest until supper time.'

Mike Russell had better watch his back when Hunter got out.

11

Laura shoved a brimming glass of chardonnay in Polly's shaking hands. 'Drink that first and then go through everything again slowly.'

'I can't.'

'Can't drink? That's not like you.' Her weak attempt at a joke fell flat. 'How about a bacon sandwich?'

'A bacon sandwich?' Big, hot tears trickled down her face. 'My wedding is off and all you can do is offer me a bacon sandwich?' Polly wailed. 'I've been a vegetarian for four years!'

Laura suspected changing the offer to cheese and pickle wouldn't help. 'I'll pop some toast in. It'll help soak up the alcohol.'

'Yes, nurse.' Polly sighed and refilled her glass. At first she glared at the plate of thick buttered toast Laura slid in front of her but picked up a slice and nibbled a tiny bite. Soon she had ploughed through the lot. Neither of them did the whole 'fading away through love of a man' thing well.

Laura flopped down on the other chair.

'I thought I knew Johnny inside out.' Polly whispered. 'This is all Hunter's fault.'

'Hunter? What's he to do with it?'

'I suppose it's not strictly his fault.'

Laura struggled to be patient.

'If I hadn't invited him to the party I'd never have found out.'

'Found out what?'

'I poked around online to discover more about Hunter so I could have a bit of fun and tease Johnny tomorrow at the party.' Polly's noisy sobs made it hard to catch her gulping words, but Laura was able to make out something about prison.

'Who's been to prison?'

'They have.'

Laura's head spun.

'Sort of.'

How could anyone sort of go to prison?

'It was one of those tough schools where desperate parents send troublesome teenagers they don't know what to do with. The name Greystone even sounds grim, doesn't it? Hunter actually runs a non-profit to help troubled youngsters unlike my dear fiancé who kept it all a secret from me. I missed finding out about that when I first checked on him because his name isn't attached to the charity unless you delve into the details of the organisation.'

'Have you asked Johnny for an explanation?'

'How could I?'

'How couldn't you? He's the man you're supposed to marry in four days. You owe him that much. Please tell me you haven't cancelled any of the wedding plans?'

'No.' Polly's protest popped out too quickly. 'Only one or two small things.'

'For instance?'

'The church.'

'I'd hardly call that a small thing.'

'Keep your hair on. The vicar wants to see us later before she agrees. Why are you so bent out of shape anyway? You never wanted me to get married in the first place.'

Talk about having her jaded views thrown back in her face. 'There's something you ought to know. I meant to ring you after I had my tea. Hunter came to see me at work this morning and someone attacked him as he was leaving. He's been admitted to the hospital with a concussion.'

'I'm trying hard to be sorry but it's not working.' Polly swiped the bottle out of Laura's reach and sloshed the dregs into her glass. 'You're knackered. I'll go back to my place and *I'll* sort this out. It's my problem.'

'But —'

' — But nothing. Before you start to lecture me I caught the bus over here so you don't have to worry about me drinking and driving. I'll let you know later if you've escaped wearing the scratchy silver dress.' Her eyes glazed with tears. 'Go to bed.'

'I will.' Now she had even more questions for her captive American.

*　*　*

Reading Johnny's text for the second time Hunter couldn't blame his fiancée for being furious. When Johnny made the choice to bury his past he had to know that one word out of place could bring it all tumbling down. Much to *his* parents' chagrin, especially his father, he was the complete opposite. They considered it demeaning to air what they considered their family's dirty laundry in public, even if Hunter's youthful struggles helped other kids with nowhere to turn.

'Why didn't you tell me?'

For a woman who couldn't have snatched more than a few hours' sleep Laura appeared as wide awake as ever.

'I assume you've heard from Johnny?'

'Yep. He popped in to see me for a

few minutes before good ole Leo ran him off.'

'Is that all I get?'

He patted the bed. 'Sit down.'

'Certainly not. That's grossly unhygienic and not something any self-respecting nurse would do.'

Hunter didn't ask about the non self-respecting ones. 'You didn't exactly brag about your ex-husband.'

'How do you . . . ? Oh God, don't tell me. The Derriford gossip machine. I should've guessed someone would relish passing on that snippet of information.' Laura sighed 'Yes, well, I'm not discussing him.' A flush of heat bloomed in her pale cheeks. 'What did Johnny do to end up in . . . that place with you?'

'You'll have to ask him. I'll spill the beans on me as much as you want.'

'Laura Williams, you know better.' Leo Painter loomed over them. 'I'll put this patient in a private room if that's what it takes to get him to rest.'

'Don't give her any grief, pal. It's my fault.'

'It most certainly is not.'

Hunter shut his mouth before he made things worse.

'I'm sorry,' Laura apologised.

'You've got one minute.' Painter strode off back to the nurses' station.

'When I get off work in the morning I'll be back to check on you.' She leaned in closer and the drift of her perfume did nothing for Hunter's equilibrium. 'Don't even think about discharging yourself and sneaking off.'

The idea hadn't occurred to him, but now she said it . . .

'I'll set Leo after you.' The mischievous threat illuminated the gold shards in her rich, brown eyes.

'That man's evil.'

'Tut, tut. You shouldn't talk about one of my colleagues that way.'

'I only said what's going through your mind.'

'Don't make that a habit.'

'Why?' Hunter stroked his fingers across her forehead. 'Is there interesting stuff rumbling around up there?' Her blush deepened and he allowed his hand to fall away. 'Good night, Ms Laura.'

'Good night, Mr McQueen.'

For a heartbeat he held onto her gaze before allowing his eyes to close, only daring to open them again when the air around him returned to reeking of its usual disinfectant.

12

Laura considered banging Polly and Johnny's stubborn heads together. He insisted that what happened in his life before they met didn't affect the man he was now or his love for her sister, but all Polly saw was a deceitful man who couldn't be trusted. She had struggled to be fair and understand both points of view, but in the end couldn't help coming down firmly on her sister's side. Laura's own marriage was based on lies and deceit so now she couldn't wrap her head around the idea that some things are best unsaid. 'Let me get this straight. The vicar persuaded you to wait until Thursday before making a decision.'

'Yes.' Polly snorted. 'But she agreed with me.'

'Not completely!' Johnny's tone was frustrated.

'What about tonight's party?' Laura glanced at the clock. 'Forty of your friends are about to descend on the Acropolis blissfully unaware that you two are on the verge of splitting up.'

'We can pretend for a couple of hours.'

Sometimes her sister was the most oblivious person on the planet. One look at the couple's strained faces and it would be obvious to everyone that something was very wrong. Laura's phone beeped and she scanned the new text message. 'Hunter's being discharged. I've got to pick him up. You're staying right here. Both of you.'

She'd say the odds were fifty-fifty whether they'd still be there when she returned.

★ ★ ★

'When we get back to your place I'm takin' a nap. They woke me all the damn time last night to make sure I woke up normally,' Hunter grumbled. 'Normally?

98

Who the hell — '

' — For God's sake stop moaning. That's normal protocol in concussion cases and for your own good.' Did she break the news about the welcome committee at her house now, or let him discover it when they arrived? 'I'm afraid your nap might have to wait.'

'Why?' Once he'd buckled his seat-belt Hunter rested his head against the window as though the effort wore him out. 'Let me guess, Johnny is being an ass and your sister's threatening to dump him.'

'Spot on.' She drove out of the car park and back into traffic. 'But you're not well and you shouldn't have to deal with that now.'

'It won't kill me to help if I can.'

Laura reached across and squeezed his hand, in the back of her mind registering the fine dark hairs shading his skin.

'In case you didn't notice the light's changed. I know y'all drive on the wrong side of the road, but I'm guessin'' your traffic lights aren't opposite too?'

Several loud blasts on a car horn startled her and she glanced in the rear-view mirror to see the driver behind her making a rude gesture involving his middle finger. With an apologetic wave she drove on. 'You're supposed to rest.'

'I appreciate your concern.' Hunter's hand rested on her thigh and the imprint of his fingers heated her skin all the way through her jeans. 'But I feel responsible.'

'Why?'

'Long story.'

Johnny's car was still parked outside as she pulled into her drive.

'You goin' in?' Hunter asked when she didn't move and Laura smiled down at his hand. 'If you let go of me I will.'

'Spoilsport.'

'That's me. Ask anyone in A&E.'

'Let's try to sort Romeo and Juliet out, minus the tragic ending.'

★ ★ ★

100

The concentration needed to follow three separate conversations on the back-end of a concussion eluded Hunter.

'Did they feed you lunch before you left the hospital?' Laura shoved a steaming mug of coffee in his hand.

'Nope.' He rushed to explain before she berated the Tamar Ward staff for incompetence. 'They offered but the lure of your top-notch cooking beat out the appetising aroma of liver and onions.'

'You clearly don't know my sister. Cooking isn't one of her many talents,' Polly scoffed and then glared between them both. 'Oh, very funny I'm sure.' Her steely gaze landed on Johnny. 'Trust you to have a delinquent for an old friend who considers it amusing that you almost tricked me down the aisle under false pretences.'

'I'll tell you anything you want to know,' Hunter offered.

'*You* will? It's his story I want.' Polly wriggled off her engagement ring and shoved it in Johnny's face. 'Last chance. Your choice. Talk or take this back.'

'We'll leave y'all to it.' He heaved himself upright, holding still for a second while the room settled around him. 'This lovely lady's goin' to take me up to bed while you spill your guts. Don't be a moron, Johnny.'

'I was going upstairs to do some ironing anyway.' Laura backed him up.

Ironing?

'I'll carry your bag.'

Hunter considered protesting but enough people were being churlish and infantile without him joining in. 'Thanks.'

'You can't go.' Polly grabbed Laura's arm.

'I most certainly can. You can't rope me in every time you and Johnny argue.' She eased away. 'I'm always here for you but the real question is if the two of you are mature enough to get married?'

'What bloody right do you have to talk to us that way? Do you seriously think we're taking marriage advice from *you*?' Johnny groaned. 'Oh hell sorry, Laura I didn't . . . I mean . . .'

102

'That's okay.' Shrugs supposedly conveyed indifference, but he guessed hers covered up a world of hurt. 'Come on, Mr McQueen. Let's get you to bed.'

'Sure thing, nurse.' He threaded his hand through her arm and steered her into the hall. 'I might come over all faint.'

'Don't lay it on too thick,' Laura hissed.

'No, ma'am.'

'Johnny was right. The idea of me giving anyone marital advice *is* a joke.'

'Don't be so damn hard on yourself. Your ex-husband is obviously a jerk. I only needed those few minutes around him to suss that one out.'

Laura sighed. 'You need to go to bed.'

Hunter considered admitting the truth about his attacker but recognised the seam of vulnerability running through her exhaustion. 'Yeah, I know.'

'I bet it's the first time you've given in that willingly.'

'At least since Charge Nurse Leo

Painter threatened me with solitary confinement.'

Laura eked out a smile. 'I'll come up with something for our dinner later if those two haven't torn my house and each other apart before then.'

'Don't fret about feeding me. I can rustle myself up a meal. You'll be off to the Greek place.'

'Why are you so sure?'

'They love each other. They'll come to their senses.'

'I really hope so.' She nibbled at her lip and gave him a strange look as if deciding how honest to be.

'I'm a good listener.'

'That's what I'm afraid of. Off you go.'

Hunter almost cracked a joke about her keeping him company but kept his mouth shut. Staying out of everyone's way was his wisest move.

13

How could a person be so dog tired they couldn't put one foot in front of the other but their brain whirred in a ceaseless round of activity?

Laura struggled to prioritise her worries. She forced to the top of the list whether the stomach virus sweeping the Plymouth area would ease off soon and, as a responsible older sister, slotted in next her concerns about Polly and Johnny. But the only problem she seemed capable of really caring about was lying on the other side of her bedroom wall.

Laura could pinpoint his scent. Clean. Warm. Overlaid with a whisper of cedar and a hint of cinnamon. She'd made a fool of herself over Mike Russell and it wasn't happening again. Raised voices and footsteps thudding up the stairs shook her back to reality.

'If you don't get rid of Hunter right

now, I will.' Polly stalked into the bedroom followed by a grim-faced Johnny. 'Poor Johnny has told me everything and we're good again but that man has to go. I refuse to have our wedding spoiled and it will be if he's there because every time I set eyes on him I'll remember what he did to my sweet man.'

'He's not well enough to come to tonight's party anyway, so why don't you go home and get ready and not worry about anything else for now?'

'But if you knew — '

' — I don't.' Laura's quiet response stopped Polly in mid-rant. 'Tomorrow you can tell me everything but tonight let's simply have fun.' An excess of ouzo, moussaka and plate smashing wasn't honestly her idea of a good time, but she'd make the best of it for her sister's sake. The relief of seeing the couple's earlier misery replaced by love rendered everything else insignificant. 'Is that okay?' she asked, attempting to dial back her habit of taking Polly's agreement for granted.

'I suppose. You will be at the Acropolis by six o'clock won't you, for the early arrivals?'

'Of course.' Who needed sleep anyway? Laura hoped she could snatch an energising nap before smartening herself up for the evening. No one would be impressed by her severe ponytail and no make-up look.

'Thanks.' Johnny kissed her cheek. 'I will be good to her. She won't regret marrying me.'

If their parents were still alive her father would lay down the law and make it clear what his youngest daughter's fiancé could expect if he didn't follow through on his promises. 'She'd better not.' Laura shooed them out and flopped on the bed. Hunter should have arrived with a government health warning.

★   ★   ★

Did she know how thin her walls were? They said people should spend the night in their guest bedrooms to make sure the bed was comfortable and the lighting was good enough. Perhaps they should also play loud music or turn on the television to see how the noise affected someone trying to sleep nearby? Polly's voice had carried only too clearly.

If you don't get rid of Hunter right now, I will. Poor Johnny has told me everything and we're good again but that man has to leave. I won't have our wedding spoiled and it will be if he's there because every time I set eyes on him I'll remember what he did to my sweet man.

Under the circumstances he understood why Johnny was trying to slant the blame over what happened to Danny Pearce in Hunter's direction. History was always nothing more than an interpretation of events. He could explain his side of the story to Laura, but what would that achieve? Doubts about her sister's choice of a husband? He and Johnny both made bad decisions as teenagers. End of story.

When Laura left for the party he'd

make himself scarce to save her the embarrassment of throwing him out. Despite the rain pelting against the glass Hunter threw open the window to push back the nightmares while he attempted to sleep. Leaving the door open would arouse Laura's suspicions and she had enough of those already. All because two decades ago a group of boys at Greystone decided he needed to be taught a lesson.

If he didn't get at least some rest he wouldn't make it very far and being hauled back into the emergency room wasn't part of his plan. He hadn't booked a return flight because when he accepted Polly's invitation he had rolled around in his mind the possibility of staying on after the wedding. The gnawing guilt over his part in the Danny Pearce's disappearance from Greystone never quite left him and needed it laid to rest. But now all he wanted was to catch the first available flight back to Knoxville.

He caught the soft click of Laura's bedroom door and jumped into bed.

No doubt she'd come in to check on him before she left which meant he needed his best imitation of heavy sleep. When his door creaked he threw in a cross between a snort and a snore for good measure and smiled as her footsteps faded away. They should award him an Oscar for that performance. She would be away for hours which meant he could afford a genuine nap. Before he turned off his phone Hunter noticed his brother had left a message a couple of hours ago. Brett always fretted over nothing so whatever it was about could wait until he got back home. The last conscious thought racing through the weariness pulling at his head was whether to leave a note behind and if so what to write. *Sorry I spoiled things. Sorry I wasn't a better houseguest. Sorry I fell for you.*

★ ★ ★

Laura stepped over a pile of broken china to reach the bar. 'I'd like a pint of

110

water please with plenty of ice.'

'Water?'

'It's the clear liquid that comes out of the taps.'

'Ah, a joker.' The barman's dark eyes sparkled and a different woman might have flirted back. His Mediterranean good looks and charming manner had attracted more than a few ribald comments from the female party guests already.

'No, simply a tired woman who isn't much of a drinker and needs to make sure the bride-to-be gets home safely.'

'One water coming up.'

She guzzled it down and the fog clouding her brain started to lift. Normally she scoffed at medical professionals who didn't take care of themselves but tonight she was no better. She was sure Hunter would give one of his slanted smiles, exposing the gold filling she'd spotted yesterday, and declare her to be simply human.

'I've got a surprise for my beautiful lady.' Johnny banged a spoon against his beer glass.

Laura had forgotten about Emily Stephens until the dark-haired Irishwoman rushed across to fling her arms around Polly and, judging by her sister's brilliant smile, at least *she* was pleased with her pre-wedding surprise. A few minutes later Johnny whisked his fiancée off for a dance and Emily materialised by Laura's side.

'How's our extremely fit Yank doing? Polly told me about Hunter's accident. If he's up for some company I'm happy to visit him. I may not be a proper nurse but I could . . . wipe his brow.'

'He needs to rest.'

'Bloody hell, Polly was right about you.'

'In what way?'

'She always said the main reason we had such a good laugh together was because you take life so seriously and don't know how to have fun.'

Laura's face burned.

'Oops. Sorry. Shouldn't have opened my big mouth.' Emily brandished an empty glass. 'Put that down to too much ouzo while I was hanging around the kitchen waiting for my big moment.'

'Don't worry. It's okay.' It really wasn't, but what could she say that wouldn't reinforce the view of her as a joyless prig? 'You go and enjoy the party. I'll see you at the wedding.' She pushed through the crowd and found Polly. 'I'm exhausted. Do you mind if I go home? No one will miss me.'

'I will — '

' — Please, Polly.' She cut her sister off. 'The weather is getting worse and I don't want to be stuck here for the night. You might think about cutting things short for everyone's safety.'

'Don't be boring. A bit of wind and rain isn't stopping *this* party.'

For the second time in five minutes she had the same label slapped on her. 'Have a good time.' She decided to treat herself to a taxi instead of waiting twenty minutes for the next bus. By the time she reached her house Laura's head throbbed and she longed to crawl into bed.

'What the devil are you doin' back?'

Hunter stood at the top of the stairs with his bag over his shoulder and guilt smeared all over his face.

'More to the point is where do you think you're going?' she responded.

14

'Out of your hair?' If he hadn't overslept Hunter would have been well on his way by now.

'Did I complain about you staying?' Colour blossomed in her cheeks. 'I mean . . . recently?'

'Nope, but Polly did. Your walls are thin.' He watched the penny drop.

'Oh, she didn't mean — '

' — Yeah, she sure did.' He made his way down to join her. 'I don't blame her. I've always been a troublemaker. Ask my parents. Especially my long-suffering father. I've never been his golden boy.' Hunter's attempt to drag out a smile ended as more of a grimace than a grin.

'I'm tired of all the innuendos and half-truths flying around. You promised to tell me your whole story.'

'I was sick and vulnerable.'

She rolled her eyes. 'Don't pull that trick.'

'You're exhausted.'

'Exhaustion comes with the job. I don't fancy coffee now but after a decent cup of tea I'll be good to go for a while. You can start talking while I make it.'

'Yes, ma'am.' A faint twinkle brightened her obvious exhaustion and it took all his strength not to give in to an impulse to hug her. Laura's unflattering plain black dress did nothing for her and the addition of a bright red scarf and matching glossy lipstick only emphasised her pallor. 'How about you change into something comfortable before we chat?' Hunter grabbed her cold hands. 'I'm not trying to flannel you, honest but you look beat and you're freezing. I'm sure I can pour hot water on a tea bag.'

'Prove it.' The husky rasp in her voice scraped at the last dregs of his self-restraint.

'You're on.' Mike Russell had already

screwed her over and she didn't need Hunter's self-preservation brand of love 'em and leave 'em romancing to rub salt in the wounds. 'Meet you in the kitchen.'

'That's a . . . fine.' She blushed and disappeared up the stairs.

A date. She almost called it a date. Probably a slip of the tongue but he liked the sound of it far too much.

★ ★ ★

As Hunter began to speak she regretted pressuring him.

'My folks used to tell people they didn't know where they went wrong with me. They brought me up the same as Brett, my older brother and he never once stepped out of line. He followed in my father's footsteps by studying law at Vanderbilt University, married his high school sweetheart and produced the expected grandchildren.' He frowned. 'Don't get me wrong I love little Caleb and Ava to death. Brett and I do okay these days when we see each other which isn't often.'

'And your parents?'

'Mom and I are sort of all right but my dad's another story . . . I guess you could say we're civil to each other. We butted heads continually when I was growing up because he insisted on things bein' done his way and came down on me like a ton of bricks every time I answered back. And I did. Continually.'

Laura felt for him. Her mum and dad never compared their two daughters and always encouraged them to follow their own paths. 'When did your troubles start?'

'Officially at eleven when I got suspended from middle school the first week for setting a fire in my homeroom teacher's trash can.' Hunter's twist of a smile spoke volumes. 'But by then I'd already become the kid other parents warned their sons and daughters to stay away from.' Lumped in with the students who were disciplinary nightmares he lived down to everyone's expectations, and the minor vandalism and end of term pranks soon escalated.

'I was in and out of the school's alternative learning centre for students who break zero tolerance rules for drug and alcohol use.' He shrugged. 'I was the life and soul of all the illicit teenage parties, my folk's drinks cabinet was fair game and I dabbled with my mom's prescription painkillers for a while.'

Now his revulsion towards the medications she'd offered made far more sense.

'That's when we came to London with my dad's job. My folks hoped the change might straighten me out but it didn't work. I'm guessin' my next stop would've been prison but in a last ditch effort Dad went against my mom's wishes and packed me off to one of these tough schools that resemble Marine Corps boot camps. The idea is they sort out wayward kids by strict discipline.' His face darkened. 'Greystone, where Johnny and I ended up, was nothing short of legalised bullying.'

Laura couldn't hide her shock.

'Said you wouldn't want to hear all this, didn't I? It's not pretty.' He fixed his bright blue eyes on her. 'You want me to keep goin'?'

Rain beat against the window and a rumble of thunder echoed in the distance. A loud crack of lightning startled her but Hunter turned white and gripped the edge of the table.

'You're not keen on storms?'

'Is anyone?'

Before she could answer the lights popped and the house plunged into darkness. 'Ouch.' Hunter grasped her hand and his fingers dug into the soft flesh.

'Sorry.'

'It's okay.'

'No, it's not I'm — '

' — I've got candles and torches but I need to find them.' Laura heard him hyperventilating. 'I'm letting go now because I need you to cup your hands in front of your mouth and breathe very slowly, preferably from your diaphragm rather than your chest.'

'I . . . can't . . . ' Hunter's panic rose.

120

'Yes you can.' She repeated her instructions and after a few agonising seconds his frantic attempts to draw in air quietened. Only when his breathing sounded normal did she dare to move, continually talking through where she was and what she was doing in an effort to reassure him.

Fumbling for the cupboard door she found the large torch she stowed there and prayed the batteries were good. 'Keep your fingers crossed.' The glare illuminated Hunter's strained features and she swept the beam away from him. With the torch set upright on the counter she found a bag of red candles and a box of matches. 'Here we go.'

'Can I help?'

'That would be great.' Laura dumped several china saucers in front of him. 'We'll have to stick them on these because my proper candle holders are packed away with the Christmas decorations in the attic.' He fumbled over lighting the first one but steadied down as the room became brighter. 'There, that's better.' She flicked off the torch.

'It sure is. Sorry. I can't handle the dark or confined spaces.' His grimace of a smile almost made her laugh but she resisted, afraid he'd take it the wrong way and think she was laughing *at* him instead of *with* him. She didn't want him to feel obliged to explain his anxieties but, considering she'd ordered him to bare his soul, what choice did they have?

★ ★ ★

Even though this part of his plan was unintentional he must have blown apart any lingering attraction Laura felt for him with that pitiful exhibition. Hunter wished the candlelight didn't enhance her loveliness quite as much. It would be easier if the gold flecks in her eyes didn't sparkle and if loose, touchable strands of hair hadn't worked free from her tight ponytail.

'What work do you do back in America?'

'Work?'

'Yes, you know the thing that pays the bills and if you're lucky you actually enjoy?' Her snappy response made him smile against his will. This woman was an expert at catching him out.

'I own a company that builds custom-designed log cabins out of repurposed wood. We source our materials from derelict buildings, mostly in the south-eastern United States.'

'Really? How did you get to doing that from . . . '

' . . . being a no good dropout?'

'I wouldn't phrase it quite that way.'

Hunter shrugged. 'Why not? It's the truth. At Greystone we did regular lessons but also had the option to take a variety of trade classes.' He fiddled with the box of matches. 'Larry Jett, the woodwork teacher didn't put up with any crap and told us all if we wanted to waste time and screw around that was our choice. He wasn't the one destined to end up unemployed, homeless and in prison.' Trying to explain Larry's influence wasn't easy. 'Jett helped me realise that without a well-rounded education I'd get nowhere and through working with my hands I discovered the redemptive power of creating something lasting.' It sounded corny but she deserved the truth.

'You're living proof there's a silver lining to every dark situation.'

'Heck, I didn't have you down for a Pollyanna.' He wished he'd kept his mouth shut when she bit her lip and her cheeks turned pink. 'Sorry. Me and compliments don't get along too well.'

'Same here. It's okay.' Her gentle smile returned.

'When my two years at Greystone were up I returned with my folks to Nashville but my father made it clear they'd be happier if I didn't hang around. I bummed around working various unskilled construction jobs before ending up in East Tennessee where I took community college classes at night until I had enough credits to complete an online business degree.' His cheeks heated. 'By then I'd hooked up with a local carpenter willing to have me as unpaid labour while he taught me all he knew.'

'Several people helped to save you but your own determination did the rest.'

'I guess.' Hunter's throat tightened.

'Polly did give you credit for trying to do the same for others. That's awesome.'

He couldn't agree without sounding full of himself.

'What's your own house like? I assume it's vastly different from my beige palace?'

The smooth change of subject proved how well she already seemed to know him. With a grin he scrolled through his phone and showed her the latest pictures he'd taken both of the inside and outside when the fall colours in the Smoky Mountains were their most vivid. He was pretty sure she'd imagined a basic cabin instead of his generously sized L-shaped design, the aged wood shaded to a soft grey and with massive windows to take full advantage of the spectacular setting. The tree-covered mountain rising in the background and stream trickling across the front of the property only added to its beauty in his opinion.

'Oh my gosh, it's stunning.'

'I'm pretty pleased with the way it turned out.' For years he'd had nothing to boast about and it still didn't sit easy with him. 'I don't know how much Johnny explained to your sister about Greystone'

'We haven't had a chance to chat yet.' Laura's eyes narrowed. 'Are you happy to put your side of the story to me first?'

One of the candles sputtered out and he dug his nails into his palm, desperate to keep from grabbing her again.

15

'Saved by the bell or rather the text message.' Laura's mobile flashed and she let Hunter read her sister's message. None of the taxi drivers would venture out as far as Polly and Johnny's flat on the other side of Plymouth because there were trees down on the main road and collapsed power lines.

Johnny's friend Rick offered to drop us at your place on his way home. All right if we crash with you tonight?

'I could hide in the attic?'

'Let's go with a no on that. It doesn't have any windows.'

'So, freaking out in the dark could turn me into a male version of Mr Rochester's crazy wife?'

It felt wrong to laugh but his warm chuckle freed her to join in.

'You'd better answer before she thinks I've brainwashed you against them.' The bitter edge to his voice wiped out the brief moment of closeness.

Laura sent off a swift reply. 'You've got maybe ten minutes before they turn up.' She watched Hunter's brain race for a few seconds before resignation settled into the creases of his face. 'It'll have to wait.'

They sat in silence with rain beating at the windows and the candles burning down.

'I'll let them in.' She grabbed the torch when she heard a car outside.

'Well, that all went pear-shaped.' Polly stumbled in over the doorstep. 'My sister bails on our party early. The bloody lights go and the restaurant turfs us all out on the street 'for our own safety'. Now I can't get home to my own bed. This better not be an omen for Saturday.'

'This gets all the bad luck out of the way.' Laura secretly crossed her fingers.

'You'd better have some booze handy because I haven't drunk nearly enough.' Polly staggered towards the kitchen. 'Oh for God's sake, are you still here?'

She lunged towards Hunter but crashed into the table and knocked over a couple of candles in the process.

Laura made a quick dive to save her tablecloth from going up in flames. 'Johnny, light a few more candles please.' She sensed Hunter's anxiety ratchet up.

'Can't you do that? I need to help Polly.'

'I'll deal with her.'

'Let Hunter take care of the candles.' Johnny sounded irritated.

'He can't.'

'Oh, sorry mate. I forgot.' Johnny looked uncomfortable and he swept his gaze over them both before doing as she'd asked while she manoeuvred Polly to sit down.

'Drink that.' She shoved a large glass of water in her sister's hand.

'I don't want to.'

'What you want is irrelevant. This is all you're getting. I'd make black coffee if we had electricity but I'm not Wonder Woman.'

'I'm not so sure about that,' Hunter quipped.

'I suggest we bring blankets and pillows down and settle in the living room for the night. They might not be able to restore the electricity anytime soon and it'll be warmer all together.'

'I'm *not* sleeping in a room with *him*.' Polly jabbed a finger at Hunter.

Where on earth had her mild-mannered sister gone? What did Johnny tell her that was so awful?

* * *

Hunter selected one of the candles from the table and stood up using every ounce of willpower to hold his hand steady. 'I'll leave y'all to it.'

'You can't,' Laura pleaded.

'I sure can.'

'But — '

' — But nothing. Give me some matches and a spare candle.'

'No, mate.' Johnny covered the box of matches with his hand. 'I'm not letting you do this.'

'For heaven's sake, what's wrong

130

with you all?' Polly scoffed. 'He's a grown man not a baby. Look at the size of him. Laura doesn't have werewolves and vampires lurking in her guest bedroom.'

Those I could deal with, thought Hunter.

'You don't get it, Poll. Hunter can't stand the dark or confined spaces and that's all my fault.'

Hunter could feel his face redden.

'He caught the brunt of things from the staff at that bloody place where our families dumped us because he refused to let them see he was scared like the rest of us.' Johnny sunk down on the chair. 'I lied to you earlier so you wouldn't realise what a jerk I used to be and not want to marry me.'

'Tell us the truth. All of it.' Laura touched Johnny's arm. 'I don't care what either of you have done but I can't stand secrets. I had enough of that in my so-called marriage.'

Polly's fierce gaze lingered on her fiancé. '*You* can forget marrying me on

131

Saturday unless you're going to treat me as an equal. I'm not a baby and I don't need protecting.'

'I didn't mean . . . I — '

' — I'll tell them if you want.' Hunter intervened. 'Any chance of a stiff drink, Laura?'

'There's some brandy.'

'Bring it on.' His razor-sharp response made everyone laugh. 'Preferably a double.'

★ ★ ★

Laura dragged out the dusty bottle from the back of a cupboard and plonked it and four glasses down on the table. She doled out generous measures and shoved one across to him. 'Get that down you and talk.'

'Yes ma'am. Good to see The Enforcer is back in business.' Hunter tipped the glass in a mock toast and gulped it down before slamming the empty glass back in front of her. 'Top it up.'

Without asking what happened to his manners she did as he asked. Laura watched enviously as Johnny pulled Polly onto his lap and wrapped his arms around her.

'There were a core group of students who bullied anyone who showed any weakness and most of the teachers were content to turn a blind eye. The others only made the occasional token protest, never enough to put a stop to it. Someone found out that Johnny hated spiders.'

'I still do.'

Laura remembered laughing with her sister when she shared a story about eradicating a particularly large, hairy spider that was freaking out her new boyfriend in the shower.

'One day the gang somehow filled his bed with spiders and removed the bulb from his bedside light so he didn't see them until they crawled all over him.' Hunter shuddered.

'What he's not telling you is that afterwards I threw my lot in with the bad crowd because I was too bloody scared of being picked on again.' Johnny sloshed another inch of brandy in his glass. 'To make sure everyone knew whose side I was on I suggested locking Hunter in a cupboard.' He clutched his head. 'We were only going to frighten him for a couple of hours but we bloody left him there all night when there was a storm and we lost power. That's why he's — '

' — worse than a damn baby when it comes to confined spaces and the dark.'

Hunter's attempt at self-deprecating humour broke Laura's heart.

'I'm certainly not standing up for what they did to you but he — ' Polly pointed to Johnny, ' — told me you were to blame when one of the other boys disappeared. Is that true?'

16

He wavered for a few seconds but the soft, fleeting stroke of Laura's fingers crumbled his last shreds of resistance.

'Johnny's talkin' about Danny Pearce.' When he spoke to the kids in his programme he never went into specifics about his time at Greystone. He used the threat to other people's privacy as his justification but now he wondered if it was only ever to protect himself and the guilt he still harboured. 'People assume all the kids in a place like that are tough troublemakers but Danny didn't fit the mould. I'm guessin' he never fitted anywhere and that's why his folks dumped him there.' Reluctantly he admitted that on one occasion he joined in when the boy was being harassed because he was weary of bearing the brunt of the staffs anger.

'You were a child yourself.'

'I was seventeen.' He didn't deserve Laura's compassion. 'Old enough to know right from wrong, although I guess none of us were great at that or we wouldn't have been at Greystone in the first place.'

'Things got out of hand one day.' Johnny took up the tale. 'When we finally stopped harassing him Danny warned us we'd be sorry in the morning.' He shrugged. 'No one saw him again.'

'There's no need to hide it any longer. We both know I saw him.' Hunter sighed. 'I watched the poor devil creep out the back door and didn't try to stop him because I thought he was better off out of there. I didn't have the guts to run away myself.' The boy's white, pinched face when he saw Hunter hovering on the stairs still haunted him. 'A few weeks later Danny sent a postcard to the school from Llandudno in Wales.'

'I'm surprised they didn't keep that under wraps.'

Hunter managed a faint smile. 'Addressed it to me, didn't he? Stuck it in an envelope so the staff couldn't see

136

who it was from. I made sure it got around.'

'I'm sorry for being so awful to you.' Polly wriggled out of Johnny's grasp. 'I need time to process all this.'

'What about our wedding?' asked Johnny, a hopeful look on his face.

'I don't know. It's still a struggle for me to wrap my head around the fact you didn't trust me enough to share all this before.'

Hunter grabbed his old friend's arm. 'Why don't we go upstairs and leave the ladies alone? You can stop the bogey man gettin' me in the dark and I'll fend off any spiders. Deal?' He hauled Johnny to his feet and gestured to the pile of spare candles. 'We'll need supplies.' Before Laura could voice her opinion, and he knew she must have one because she did about everything else, he threw her a warning glance. For only the second time since they met she conceded.

★ ★ ★

137

Laura leaned her head against the cold window as if staring at the dark streetlights would magic the electricity back on. Far past normal exhaustion she knew if she tried to follow Polly's example and fall asleep it would be a dismal failure. Her sister hadn't needed much persuasion to wait until the morning to talk and cuddled up on the floor wrapped in Laura's duvet hugging her pillow the exact same way she'd done as a child.

Hunter and Johnny's story ran through her head in a continual loop.

'The goddamn rain's finally stopped.' Hunter's raspy whisper startled her.

'What the — '

' — Sorry.' He hung back in the doorway, shielding the light from the mobile phone in his hand. 'I guessed she'd have already been asleep.' He gestured towards Polly. 'She could barely hold her eyelids open.'

'And me?'

His smile deepened in the flickering shadows. 'You're like me and your brain's too wired to sleep. Johnny went out like the flamin' lights.'

'You should be resting. Your head must be hurting still.'

'It's been better but I'll survive.'

Laura shivered. 'I'd kill for a hot drink right now.'

'I can't conjure one out of thin air but I give pretty damn good hugs if you fancy takin' the chance?'

Hadn't she taken enough chances where Hunter McQueen was concerned already? He set down the light on the bookcase allowing them to see each other's faces without disturbing Polly. With his hair untied and wearing baggy sweatpants and a loose, dark jumper he appeared more vulnerable, less imposing. Without a word she rested her head against his chest allowing the familiar hints of cedar and cinnamon to tease her senses while his comforting arms wrapped her in a tight embrace.

'Warmin' up?'

Laura met his obvious amusement. Of course he'd nailed her reaction to the heat radiating from him. 'Tease.'

Hunter brushed away a couple of stray curls from her face and a slow smile inched down to linger around his mouth.

'Isn't this too dark for you?'

'You keep the fears at bay.'

There were so many more questions she needed answered but the only thing that mattered right now was how soon he'd kiss her.

* * *

Since the grey, rainy day when he first set eyes on Laura, dripping wet but spirited as hell, he'd ached to kiss her and now he wasn't waiting another second. He fought to keep the kiss gentle until a faint moan escaped the back of her throat. It didn't help when her fingers explored under the hem of his jumper and stroked his hot, tight skin.

'You'd better stop there unless . . . '

'Unless what?' Her husky whisper unravelled another layer of restraint.

With a pop the lights flashed back on and instead of giving thanks for the genius electricity workers, he could have groaned out loud. The only consolation came from the matching disappointment in Laura's dark eyes.

Polly jerked awake. 'What are you two . . . oh, daft old me.' She smacked her head. 'I can't believe I didn't see it before.'

Johnny stumbled into the room. 'What happened to you? I woke up and you'd disappeared'

'Mr McQueen sneaked down to make a move on my sister.'

'That figures. I saw it coming in Princetown.'

'Princetown? What on earth are you talking about?' Polly waved her engagement ring in Johnny's face. 'The whole truth.'

'Why don't I put the kettle on?' Laura offered. 'I heard the central heating kick back on so the house should soon warm up.'

Hunter could think of more entertaining ways to stay toasty.

Five minutes later they sat around

the kitchen table in a complete déjà vu moment except with mugs of tea instead of brandy while Johnny poured out the whole story of Thursday's accidental meeting at the pub in Princetown.

'They were practically drooling over each other.' Johnny chuckled.

'Don't be daft,' Laura blurted out. 'He'd only arrived the day before. Who on earth do you think I am?'

'A lonely woman in need of a good man.'

Hunter waited for Laura to give his old friend a tongue lashing but she stared down at the table and said nothing.

'We're going upstairs to talk.' Polly took Johnny's arm and flashed a cheeky smile. 'Let's leave the lovebirds to it.'

Nobody contradicted her.

'Do you think they'll sort it out?' Hunter asked when they were alone.

'Yes, I do. They've got . . . something I never had with Mike.' Laura's mono-tone voice betrayed her deepest emotions more than tears would have done. 'Do you know what she said when I asked why they didn't simply live together? Polly told me they *wanted* to be legally tied because they didn't want to make it easy to leave.' Her dull eyes fixed on him. 'I won't ever take that risk again.'

The line in the sand. There it was. He could remind her they'd only known each other a few days and weren't at the point of needing this conversation but sensed she *did* need it. If he could expose Mike for the jerk he was without humiliating Laura that would be some sort of payback for what the man had done to her.

'Johnny was right in a way.' Laura cleared her throat. 'I *am* lonely sometimes but what he doesn't understand is that it's heaps better than my miserable marriage ever was.'

Hunter had been around enough bullies to recognise one in Mike Russell, white coat or no white coat.

'I like you. Really like you.' A rush of colour bloomed in her neck. 'But I've nothing to offer . . . that way.'

You do but you're afraid and I don't

143

blame you. We're more alike than you realise. He didn't say the words he was thinking.

'Maybe it would be for the best if I move on,' Hunter said. 'I'll grab a couple hours sleep and leave later if that's okay?'

'Of course.' Laura's resigned tone tore at him but he needed to do the right thing for once and leave her alone. He'd learned the hard way what making the wrong choices did for a person's life.

Without another word he left the room, shutting the door behind him.

17

Laura stripped Hunter's bed and caught the last hints of his scent nestled deep in the crumpled white sheets. After they saw each other at the wedding on Saturday he'd fly back to Tennessee and that should be the end. The problem was she suspected she'd hear his deep rumbling laughter in every room and taste him on her mouth, remembering the one kiss they hadn't been able to resist. If the lights hadn't come back on . . .

'Where's Romeo?' Polly breezed in.

'If you mean Hunter, he's gone.'

'Why?'

'Uh, maybe because that was always the agreement.' Laura struggled to sound unconcerned. 'You asked me to take care of him until after the party and promised he'd do his own thing then until the wedding.'

'But I thought — '

' — Well, you thought wrong,' she snapped. 'I'm back on duty first thing tomorrow morning so I need to get my house straight and do some food shopping.' Polly's smile faded. 'Sorry, I don't mean to be . . .'

'A cow?'

'I wasn't *that* bad.'

'Moo, moo.' Polly teased. 'In case you're interested, Johnny and I had a real heart-to-heart talk. He's never told me much about his family before, only that his parents passed away when he was young and he didn't have any brothers or sisters. It turns out he got sent to live with a childless aunt and uncle in Bristol who couldn't cope when he turned into a rebellious, mouthy teenager. They sent him to Greystone because they didn't know what else to do with him.' She flashed a bright smile. 'Anyway I don't want to harp on about all that now because some of us have a wedding to organise. We've checked and the roads are clear so we'll get a taxi back to the flat. I can hardly meet the florist wearing this.' Last night's red sequined dress looked somewhat the worse for wear in the harsh morning light. 'I still can't get my head around you letting Hunter go. Didn't you see the way he looked at you?'

I felt it all the way to my toes. 'Hunter understands where I'm coming from.'

'I doubt that. I know your divorce was rough, but surely you aren't going to be a nun for the rest of your life?'

This was the perfect chance to share the whole truth of her marriage, but at the last second the protective older sister gene kicked back in. 'I'm fine. Off you go and worry about nothing more serious than flowers and wedding cake. If there's anything I can do to help let me know.'

'You said that with a straight face. I'm impressed.'

'I mean it.' Laura reached for Polly's hand. 'I would do *anything* to make Saturday the happiest day of your life.' She smiled. 'Anything except invite Hunter McQueen back here and into my bed.'

'Spoilsport.'

'That's me. I didn't get my Enforcer nickname by being agreeable.'

'The taxi's on its way.' Johnny strolled in and offered Polly her coat. 'Thanks for everything, Laura.'

'You're welcome.'

'Where's Hunter?'

'Gone.' Polly answered before Laura had a chance.

He glanced between them both but wasn't stupid enough to pursue the subject.

A few minutes later Laura fought to be grateful for her quiet house.

★ ★ ★

The three-mile hike helped his lingering headache and should have given Hunter a healthy appetite but he stared listlessly at his cream tea. If Laura was sitting across the table from him wearing her funny reindeer hat they'd be arguing about something silly and wolfing down their food together. It had been a lousy choice to return to Dartmoor and attempt to finish their day out. Usually his relationships with women foundered around the two-month point because they started to 'expect' things from him. Things he couldn't live up to. But Laura? He suspected that he would have done whatever she asked to keep the glittering twinkle in her dark, serious eyes.

'Would you like to take the leftovers home with you?' The waitress pointed at the neglected scones. 'It's a shame to waste them.'

'Sure that would be great, if it's not too much trouble.'

'None at all my 'andsome.' She bustled away and soon he found himself standing outside the café holding a white paper bag.

I popped you in a tub of cream and one of strawberry jam. There's an extra scone too because it's getting late in the day and we won't sell them now. They'll only be thrown out to feed the birds, the waitress had said.

That's probably what would happen with them anyway, but he hadn't told her that. Hunter shoved the bag of food inside his backpack and headed for the bus stop. He had stirred up enough trouble for Johnny and couldn't stick to his original plan to bail out before Saturday's big day. The fact it gave him the opportunity to see Laura one last time was either a bonus or the worst thing ever; he couldn't be sure. On the way back from Dartmoor last time he distracted her by asking for some details about the wedding She had winced and described her pale silver, heavily sequinned bridesmaid's dress. *It makes me look like the Shard building in London when it's all lit up.* To keep her bare arms warm in the old granite church there was also a short white feather jacket, which she claimed made her resemble a swan caught in a strong gale of wind.

This morning the crisp, dry weather allowed him to glimpse Dartmoor in a more appealing light but now the drizzle was rolling back in. Hunter pulled up the hood of his coat and smiled at the idea of Laura being proud of him. Damn it, why couldn't he stop thinking of the woman? He jerked the hood back down. If he caught pneumonia at least he knew where to track down a good nurse.

★   ★   ★

The first slivers of light eked into the morning sky as Laura hurried towards the hospital from the bus stop. She couldn't stop wondering where Hunter had spent the night despite the fact he was an intelligent, grown man with enough money and command of the English language to have secured a hotel room.

Talk about books and their covers. No one looking at Hunter would guess the extent of his crippling anxieties. Professionally, she longed to encourage him into therapy and treatment for the PTSD he clearly suffered from but the suggestion couldn't come from her. While she ran through a few names in her head as to who might be able to help Hunter, she almost bumped into someone coming out of the back door of the A&E department.

'Well, if it isn't my favourite nurse.' Mike swaggered to a halt in front of her. 'Has your Yankee boyfriend gone back where he belongs? Hopefully he got the hint he wasn't wanted around here.'

'What business is it of yours?' Laura's heart raced. Years ago that same reaction would happen in a good way every time the handsome surgeon sought her out. At first she put his arrogance and need for control down to the pressures of his job but that was before they married and she discovered the full extent of his domineering personality.

'You'll always be my business, Laura.' He captured her chin in a tight grasp and the breath caught in her throat.

'Tell that to your barmaid.'

'We all make mistakes.' Mike's thin lips curled in a sneer. 'Except for you.'

From the distance of time she saw how he had placed the blame for the failure of their marriage on her alone because his conceit wouldn't allow him to admit any fault on his part. 'I'm on duty in five minutes. I need to go. Please move out of my way.'

He loomed over her. 'Are you going to make me?'

'You really don't want to find out.'

Mike yanked her into his arms, brought his mouth crashing down on hers and forced his tongue between her lips.

You asked for it. Laura brought her knee up between his legs at the perfect angle to exact the most damage and sent him crumpling to the ground.

'Bitch.'

She crouched down and hissed in his ear. 'Don't ever come near me unless it's in a professional capacity. I'm never going to be your victim again.' Laura hurried towards the door with her legs shaking so badly they barely functioned. In the ladies' loos she splashed cold water on her face and tidied back her hair.

Hopefully he got the hint he wasn't wanted here.

Mike's words sunk in and everything fell into place like the last pieces in a complicated jigsaw puzzle. She matched up her ex's snide remarks when he caught her with Hunter with her houseguest's supposed inability to describe his attacker. God, she must be stupid. The question was what to do with the information now?

18

If Hunter had calculated right Laura should get off her third twelve-hour shift in a few minutes. In his dreams she threw herself at him and admitted she'd made a dreadful mistake by letting him leave but as a pragmatic man he would take being spoken to again as a major achievement.

He'd passed the time since they parted ways with aimless sightseeing because he couldn't come to a decision about whether or not to track down Danny Pearce. After his Dartmoor expedition on Sunday afternoon the weather trundled downhill again. He tramped around the city on Monday, checked out the Barbican, photographed the Mayflower steps and feigned an interest in the aquarium. Tuesday he ventured down into Cornwall and made it all the way to Land's End. At least he assumed he did because

155

the signs said so but through the lashing rain and gale force winds it'd been impossible to see past his feet. This morning when it was another grey, dreary morning and his boots were still drying on top of the radiator he'd sprung his bright idea on Polly. Her dubious reaction only made him more determined to see it through. After he got everything set up he took a long hot shower, shaved, left his clean hair loose and slipped into fresh clothes, choosing the blue jeans and white shirt that had caught Laura's eye the other day.

'This is costing you a bomb, mate.' The taxi driver laughed. 'I hope she's worth it.'

'She sure is.' Hunter had considered catching the bus or calling one of the ride-share options but both would give Laura a better chance to bail out on him. He reckoned having a warm taxi ready for her to jump into amped up his chance for success. Keeping his eyes on the exit he leapt from the car as soon as she stepped outside.

156

'Fancy a ride home?'

'Dare I ask what you're doing here?'

Hunter flashed what he hoped was a winning smile and a miniscule crack appeared in Laura's grim expression. 'How does a long hot bath, homemade beef stroganoff, a nice bottle of merlot and a foot rub sound?'

'I assume that's a hypothetical question?' Her eyebrows knotted together. 'In theory it would be close to perfect but — '

' — Trust me.' He gestured towards the taxi.

'Where are we going . . . if I'm foolish enough to play along with this daft game?'

'Your house.'

Laura's cynical laugh wasn't encouraging. 'Well we certainly won't find any of those at my place except for the bath, and it won't be that long or the water will go cold.'

'I guess the length of the soak in the bath might be exaggerated . . . I didn't have time to redo your plumbing but the rest are definitely a go.'

'What are you up to?'

'Just tryin' to spoil you, and maybe . . . we'll see.' He took a risk and reached for her hand. 'How about we sort this out in the dry?'

'You are an exasperating man.' Laura sighed. 'Fine. I'm too tired to argue.'

'Hurry up love, or he'll need to take out a mortgage to pay me.'

She shook her head at the driver's jovial comment. 'How long have you been waiting?'

'Long enough.' Hunter interrupted and steered her towards the car. So far, so good.

* * *

She leaned her head against the window because she was too weary to sit upright and the other unacceptable option was Hunter's tempting, broad shoulder. The backseat of the car allowed no room to get away from the warm, familiar scents which always surrounded him. Catching her out this way he'd destroyed her careful plan to make it through the week before facing him one last time on Saturday. Why hadn't she guessed this unpredictable man wouldn't accept an easy brush off?

'Here we go. Enjoy your evening.' The driver winked at Hunter in a matey way, clearly thinking he was in luck.

Talk about being flat-out wrong, especially after this morning's confrontation with her ex-husband. Laura jumped out, slammed the car door and fumbled for her keys in the bottom of her bag. Before she could pull them out Hunter sprinted to the door and stuck a key in the lock.

'Where did you get that from?'

'Polly.'

'Polly?' *Wait until she got her hands on her devious sister.* The appetising waft of warm air and fragrant beef drifting out sent Laura's blood pressure soaring. 'Have you been in my house while I've been out?'

Hunter's smile faltered.

'Why does everyone think they know better when it comes to my life? You should ask Mike Russell what happens to men who try to force me to do anything against my will.' Laura gave him no chance to respond. 'Oh, that's right he might punch you again and send you back into Leo Painter's tender hands.'

His blue eyes turned dark as midnight. 'How did you . . . ?'

'I bumped into Mike this morning and he asked whether my American 'friend' had gone back where he belongs. He added that you'd hopefully got the hint you weren't wanted here,' Laura scoffed. 'Putting two and two together didn't need a maths degree.'

'You said somethin' about him forcing you. If he — '

' — I'm capable of looking after myself, thank you very much. I kneed him where it hurts and, with my medical knowledge, I'd say his little barmaid will be out of luck tonight.'

'Good. I was goin' to tackle him myself but I guess I don't need to now.'

Against her will Hunter's tentative smile amused her.

'Will you give me a break? Please?'

'Why?'

'Because I can't leave after the wedding not knowing if there's a chance we — '

' — I told you before there can never be any sort of 'we' and I meant it.' Laura struggled to suppress her frustration. 'You need to get that through your thick skull.'

'It's not that thick. You've seen the X-rays.'

The burst of laughter erupted before she could crush it. She slumped down on the sofa and kicked off her shoes. 'Oh I give up. For God's sake, open the bloody bottle of wine, pour me an outsize glass and feed me.'

★   ★   ★

'Yes, ma'am.' He hoped she wouldn't throw him out after he'd washed the dishes later. Hunter carried two large

161

glasses of wine back into the living room and she snatched hers from his hand.

'I hope this isn't some expensive vintage I'm supposed to appreciate because I'm in the mood to get tipsy as fast as possible.'

'Nah, it was on special at your grocery store.'

'You can sit down. I won't bite. At least not until the food appears.'

'I need to get back on chef duty. Are you happy to eat in here?'

'Try to prise me from this comfy sofa and see what happens.'

He disappeared and brought back the food.

Laura's first large forkful of stroganoff was followed by another and another until her plate was clean. 'That was incredible. Are you seriously claiming you made this yourself?' She didn't attempt to hide her scepticism. 'Don't waste time lying. I always buy the supermarket ready meal deals. You can't beat getting two mains, a pudding and bottle of plonk for a tenner.'

Hunter didn't have a clue what she was rambling on about but got the impression she was dubious about his cooking skills. If he admitted to making the pasta from scratch she definitely wouldn't believe him. 'I'm done lying to you. I made it all. Okay?' Her wide-eyed unguarded glance set loose the coil of arousal that had tugged at him since the moment they met.

'Oh.' Laura's low, husky whisper finished him.

'Last time we were interrupted by the lights comin' back on.' Later he might regret this, or in the next few seconds if she slapped his face, but he trailed his finger along her jaw and lingered against her mouth. 'It's your call now.'

Laura wound her hands around his neck to draw him closer. Her soft lips brushed over his and the hints of lush, ripe fruit from the wine they'd drunk heightened his senses. She fumbled with his shirt buttons but he resisted helping her. No way did he intend for her to turn around later and say he'd pressured her in the heat of the moment. Hunter's cautiousness lasted until her fingers stroked his burning skin.

'Are you sure about this? Only a minute ago you said — '

' — and I meant it, but I'm offering this. Now. Only this.' The colour rose in her cheeks. 'Of course if you don't want to . . . '

'You can't believe that.' If he said too much the words would come back to bite him later. 'Here or upstairs?' Not the most eloquent offer he'd ever made a woman.

'Here . . . first.' Laura's eyes sparkled. 'If it's not too beige for you?'

'I'm becomin' a real fan of beige.' Making her laugh broke through the last of his reservations. Offers could be renegotiated at a later date.

19

Laura met Hunter's full-on smile as he set a loaded breakfast tray on the bed in front of her while telling herself not to get too used to this. 'Aren't you just the perfect man?' she said wryly.

'Far from it.' He jumped back in with her and held out a rasher of crispy bacon for her to bite. 'Simply a decent cook and hopefully decent . . . in other ways too.'

Morning-afters were tricky, at least from what she could remember. There hadn't been anyone since Mike and before she got married there were only a couple of casual boyfriends at university who didn't last long enough for it to be an issue. Mike always claimed her feminine curves made her useless in bed and turned him off but last night she realised that was his problem and nothing to do with her.

Hunter had helped her to discover she was a deeply passionate woman and she was grateful to him for that.

Grateful? If a man thought about her that way she'd be furious.

'Eat up before it goes cold.'

She poked a fork at her perfectly scrambled eggs and blinked away a rush of tears. Life would return to cold and ordinary when Hunter left.

'You aren't working again until after the wedding, right?'

Laura nodded, too choked to speak.

'I guess I'm tempting fate but today's weather forecast is pretty decent. On Sunday I tried to finish our Dartmoor day out but couldn't eat a cream tea on my own.' His fake sad face eked a smile out of her. She heard all about the waitress who forced the leftovers on him and the hungry stray dog who benefitted. 'How about we head that way for an energetic hike before stuffing ourselves with scones and tea?' A curtain of black silky hair fell over his face and she wound a long strand around her fingers.

'Later. Move the tray or we'll make a mess of the bed.'

Hunter grinned, dumped the tray on the floor and pushed her down on the pillows. 'We're gonna make a mess of it anyway, sweetheart.'

★   ★   ★

Standing together at the top of Wind Tor they soaked in the stunning view spread out around them where the stark winter landscape, a stunning patchwork of bronzes and greys, was interspersed with pops of purple heather glowing in the pale sunshine. 'Thank you. I needed this,' she said.

He brought Laura around to face him, buffeting her from the stiff breeze with his solid body. 'It's me who should be thankin' you. On my own this was . . . a walk, nothing more. Sharing changes it. Changes everything, doesn't it?'

'Yes, not always in a good way but this is.'

During the night, drowsy and satiated she'd opened up more about her marriage and now he had a clearer picture of why she'd become so buttoned up. She brushed off his attempt to sympathise by saying he hadn't had an easy time either and that life wasn't always fair.

'Ready to head back down?' He patted his stomach. 'I don't think I'll have a problem eating that cream tea today.'

'Worked up an appetite, have you?' Laura's tinkling laughter sounded girlish and free.

'I sure have. You make a man mighty hungry.' The suggestive double entendre behind his comment made her blush. Playing along was the only way to hold onto her for now. 'Race you.' Hunter took off running, but she easily sprinted past him with the reindeer ears on her hat flapping in the wind.

By unspoken consent they kept the conversation light while relishing their cream tea and the quiet drive back to her house.

'This is where we started.' He pointed to the takeaway cartons from the Chinese restaurant spread out over the bed later on.

'Not quite. I'd say we've moved on a little since that.' Laura stroked his bare chest. 'I'm afraid I can't see you tomorrow.'

'Can't or won't?'

'Can't. Polly has booked us a sisterly bonding session at a local spa.' She screwed up her face. 'I'll be manicured, pedicured and massaged within an inch of my life by the time we're through.'

Hunter stroked his hand down her thigh. 'I could be extremely appreciative of the results tomorrow night.'

'I think it might be more sensible if you leave in the morning.' The gold sparks in her eyes faded. 'I'll be busy and you'll be heading back across the pond after the wedding anyway. There's no point in dragging it out.'

'Draggin' it out?' His raised voice made her stiffen against him.

'I didn't mean it the way you're

thinking. You know I've loved . . . I mean enjoyed being . . . with you. Oh, this isn't coming out right.'

He tossed the covers away and dragged his clothes back on. 'There *is* no *right* way to say I'm good enough to share your bed for a few nights as long as I leave like an obedient puppy when you're through with me.'

★ ★ ★

This was what she'd dreaded. What was it with her and men? She never got it quite right. Mike turned out to be an unfaithful, possessive bully and now Hunter expected too much despite her warnings.

'I told you I was offering this. Only this.' Laura's voice rose. 'What part of that didn't you understand?' Her cruel words made him flinch but softening wasn't an option. Not after she'd fought hard for her independence.

'Oh I understood.' His raspy whisper tortured her. 'I guess it was foolish to think last night affected you as much as it did me.' Hunter's deep sigh resonated through the room. 'I sure got that wrong.'

No, you didn't, but for my own peace of mind it's my turn to lie, she thought to herself. 'The sex was good. No, better than good. Great.' Laura forced herself to smile. 'You're a very considerate lover.'

'Considerate?' He glowered. 'That's damning praise if ever I heard it.'

'Would you prefer inconsiderate?'

He tugged on his battered cowboy boots and straightened to his full height. 'Don't fret I'll steer clear of you at the wedding and then get out of your hair for good.'

She knew he would still be in her mind and heart but stared down at the bedcovers until his heavy footsteps thudded down the stairs and the front door slammed shut on his way out.

Large, hot tears inched down her face and she ruthlessly brushed them away. Nothing was going to spoil Polly's wedding if Laura had to stitch on a permanent smile for the next two days.

She refused to ring Polly for a good moan because her sister was quite rightly floating on a magical fluffy wedding cloud far above mundane concerns. Hopefully by the morning she could hide her feelings well enough to fool Polly, but it wouldn't happen tonight while her confrontation with Hunter was so raw.

A tease of cinnamon reached her nose and she ripped the sheets and pillowcases off the bed. Next she took the longest, hottest shower her inadequate plumbing could manage before choking down a slice of cheese on toast with a large mug of sweet tea. By seven o'clock she sat on the sofa and grimaced at the dull, beige walls. With no solid plan in mind she checked the opening times of the nearest DIY shop and found there was an hour left until it closed. Laura replaced her pyjamas with old jeans and a thick black jumper, broke the speed limit and then had to grit her teeth while an annoying salesman tried to convince her that greys, neutrals and earth tones were this year's popular colours.

She'd had neutral up to her eyeballs. If she didn't have the guts to take a chance on Hunter, she could at least shake up this aspect of her life.

Back home she almost wrenched her back trying to shift the living room furniture into the middle of the room. After covering up her carpet with old sheets she prised open the paint tin. Laura stuck the brush in and sucked in a deep breath before painting the first swath of sunshine yellow on the wall. She'd heard the old song about washing a man out of your hair but wasn't sure if painting one out worked the same way. By the morning she should know.

20

Hunter worked the benefits of being a conspicuous stranger to the utmost and used his affable, southern charm on the barman. A couple of pints and a shepherd's pie later Adam Taylor was his new best friend.

'There's Kiki now, ask her yourself if I'm spinning a yarn.' Adam nodded towards a tired, washed-out, very pregnant blonde woman easing herself into a chair by the fire. 'We worked together here for about six months. In this job you get good at sizing up people but she still fell for Russell's chat up lines. I don't care if he's someone high and mighty at the hospital, the man's still a wanker.'

'You won't get any argument from me on that score.' Hunter rubbed at a tender spot on the back of his head. 'I don't want to freak her out.'

'I'll take her a fresh drink and put in

a word for you.'

'You're a good guy.'

The colour rose in his cheeks. 'She deserves better.'

'She sure does.' He watched while the barman took Kiki an orange juice and a frown crossed her face. Finally she glanced his way and shrugged.

Adam cleared a few glasses from the tables and returned behind the bar. 'Take these.' He thrust a bag of crisps at Hunter. 'Prawn cocktail flavour. She can't get enough of them.'

'Seriously? You Brits are weird.'

'Says the man who probably eats maple syrup on his sausages.'

'With a stack of buttermilk pancakes? Nothin' better.'

'Weird is as weird does.' Adam grinned before his good humour faded away. 'If there's anything I can do to help screw one over on the good doctor, let me know.'

'I sure will and thanks again.' Swinging the bag of crisps in his hand Hunter prepared to put 'Operation Sink Mike Russell' into action.

★ ★ ★

At the shop there were a hundred shades of yellow and she'd managed to select one with a distinctly green tinge. It reminded her of someone who'd eaten too much ice cream and was on the verge of throwing up. Not exactly the look she'd been aiming for.

She flopped down on the sofa, kicked off her shoes and rested her feet on the coffee table. The doorbell startled her out of a light doze and she hurried out to discover Johnny on the doorstep brandishing a bottle of whisky.

'Is Hunter around?'

'Uh, no.'

'Mind if I come in and wait for him?'

When Johnny discovered the truth it would mean Polly would too, and then she'd be treated to a 'I-warned-you-not-to-mess-up' lecture. 'He's gone and he won't be back.'

'You mean tonight or . . . ?'

'Not ever as far as I know.' Laura

176

forced on a smile. 'We had a . . . disagreement. He's still coming to the wedding though.'

'Pity.' Johnny looked uncomfortable. 'About the disagreement I mean, not the wedding.'

'Did you want him for something in particular?'

He studied her for a moment. 'Do you fancy a drink?'

A prickle of unease stirred inside her. 'Please tell me nothing's wrong with you and Polly?'

'No. We're good.'

The sense that he needed to talk to someone lingered. 'You can still come in. I could do with a break.'

'What the bloody hell have you been doing?' He halted in the doorway.

'Painting. What does it look like?'

'You seriously want to know?'

'The colour wasn't quite what I had in mind, but it's growing on me.' Laura folded her arms over her chest, curiously defensive about her new colour scheme if four walls could be described as an actual plan.

'It's . . . a change.'

'Yes, well, that's what I need.'

'Sit down and I'll pour us both a stiff drink.'

With no energy to object she lay back on the sofa and closed her eyes while he fumbled around in the kitchen.

'Get that down you.' Johnny shoved a glass in her hand. 'Do you want to tell me what's up with you and Hunter?'

'It can wait. You go first.'

He exhaled a long, weary sigh. 'It's about Danny Pearce.'

*　*　*

'Tell me if I've got this right.' Hunter had received a few filthy looks from the locals when Kiki burst into tears and wouldn't stop sobbing. 'You agreed to Mike's request for a DNA test but when it came back positive he accused you of tricking him and took you to a fellow doctor who performed a different, invasive paternity test which could

178

have resulted in you losing the baby?'

'Yes, well that's what he wanted, isn't it?' Kiki's soft blue eyes swam with tears. 'But that test came out positive too.' She plucked at the frayed sleeve of her baggy grey cardigan. 'He claims he'll make me regret it if I put his name on the birth certificate. My dad says to keep my mouth shut because Mike offered me a ton of money and I need it for the baby.'

The sheer arrogance of the man stunned him. 'Ultimately it's your call, but what if he does this to another woman?' Kiki opened her mouth to protest but slammed it shut again. 'Should he be allowed to continue practising medicine?' Hunter wasn't certain how hard to press. 'Would you consider talking to a lawyer?'

Her eyes flared. 'I couldn't do that. I . . . love him.'

'Still?'

'He's my baby's father.'

'Don't you owe your baby better than a father who would risk its life?'

'You got me all mixed up. He only

needed to be sure, that's all.' She stumbled to her feet.

'If you change your mind, here are my contact details.' Hunter pressed one of his business cards into Kiki's hand. He hauled his backpack on his shoulder before he realised he'd nowhere to stay the night. Perhaps he'd wander past Laura's house to check if her lights were still on.

And what are you goin' to do if they are? What part of being thrown out didn't you get, moron?

21

'Couldn't this wait until after the wedding?' Laura ventured.

'No, because Hunter's leaving and I'll be tied up with my honeymoon.' Johnny cracked a smile. 'Not literally, because Polly's not that way inclined. The whole *Fifty Shades* thing passed us by.'

Her doorbell jangled again, startling them both.

'Do you want me to check who it is?'

'Don't be daft,' Laura scoffed. 'A bona fide axe-murderer would hack the door down not ring the bell.' She hurried to open the door and the last person she'd expected to see again anytime soon stood on the step. 'Were your ears burning?'

'Should they be?'

'Who was . . . hey, Hunter. Just the man I was looking for.' Johnny's relief was palpable. 'Get in out of the rain for Christ's sake.'

'Is it raining?'

'It's always raining.' Laura sighed. 'Do what he says.'

'Yes, ma'am.'

When he stepped into her living room his eyes brightened.

'No more beige palace.' Laura couldn't help her nervous laugh. 'At least not in here.'

'You've been busy,' Hunter said with a hint of amusement.

'Whisky?' Johnny held up the bottle.

'Do I need it?'

'It might not hurt.'

Hunter raised an eyebrow at them both and took the drink Johnny shoved in his hand. 'What's up?'

'Thanks to you I couldn't resist checking up on Danny Pearce today.' Johnny's forehead settled into deep furrows. 'I'd managed to avoid thinking about him for years until now. Not sure what that says about me.'

'Why don't we all sit down?' Laura

suggested and returned to the sofa. When Hunter joined her she didn't stop to think and reached for his cold hand.

★ ★ ★

He couldn't get his head around Johnny's resentment. Not a single day passed since he left Greystone when he didn't wonder about Danny Pearce. Had the postcard even been genuine? Assuming it was from him, how did his life turn out? Did Hunter make the right choice in letting the other boy go from Greystone that night? Johnny's choice to whitewash over that part of his life had come back to haunt him, and he couldn't bring himself to apologise for that.

'Believe it or not I found a Daniel Pearce living in Cornwall. Take a look at this. There's no doubt it's him.' Johnny brandished his phone in Hunter's face and the picture leaping out at him was an older version of the scrawny boy they both remembered.

'So, what are we gonna to do?'

A hint of wariness shadowed Johnny's face. 'I guessed that's how you'd react.'

'Well yeah.' Hunter frowned. 'You're in too surely?'

'Yesterday I was all fired up and I came around here full of good intentions . . . ' Johnny trailed a finger around the rim of his empty glass. 'I'm starting a new chapter in my life in a couple of days. Maybe it's best to leave the past alone.'

'How do you think Polly will react when she finds out?' Laura chipped in. 'She will you know.'

'She'll be pissed.'

'It won't be easy,' Hunter admitted, 'but we've — '

' — got to discover the truth.' Johnny sighed. 'I know.'

'You fret about the wedding, and I'll take this on.'

'Aren't you leaving on Sunday?'

'I could hang around. The week you're away on honeymoon gives me plenty of time to do more research.' He caught Laura's surprise. 'If that's okay? I didn't mean to take it for granted . . . I can find somewhere else to stay if you'd prefer it?'

'Don't be silly.'

Her cautious smile made Hunter want to punch the air with joy.

'I'm really leaving this time. I'll see you both on Saturday.' Johnny winked. 'Be careful, mate. She'll have a paint-brush in your hand before you know where you are.'

He'd paint the house from top to bottom if that's what it took to make her happy.

'Ha! I can tell by the look on your face you're screwed.' Johnny grinned at him. 'A bloody lost cause.'

Hunter thought that sounded pretty damn good to him.

A few minutes later he wrapped his arms around her and discovered that Laura's soft floral scent overcame the smell of fresh paint.

'You were brave to come back.'

'Did you honestly expect me to stay gone?'

'I was afraid you might.' Her confession made him smile. 'My luck with men isn't exactly stellar.'

If he brought up the subject of Kiki now Laura might misunderstand why he'd gathered the nerve to return. Tomorrow morning was soon enough to throw another challenge into the mix.

22

The rigid set of Hunter's shoulders. The way his smile reached his eyes the fraction of a second after the twitching of the corners of his mouth. Everything pointed towards him keeping something from her again.

'Somethin' wrong?'

'You tell me.'

'I thought it could wait but as usual you're right. It can't.' He gave a wry smile. 'It's not us. Promise.'

'Then what is it?'

'I reckon this needs a mug of hot tea to hand.'

Laura couldn't help laughing. 'Have we converted you to the medicinal benefits of a decent tea bag and boiling water?'

'Sure have.'

'Why don't you put your things back upstairs while I'll stick the kettle on?'

She hesitated. 'You might as well put them in my room.'

'You're sure?'

'Yes.' Whatever the problem was they'd sort it together and move on from there. She scrolled through the latest messages on her phone while she waited for the water to boil and noticed several missed texts from Henry. She'd made it clear she wasn't working again until Monday, so why was he bothering her now? As she read through them a chill shivered down her spine. 'Is this what you didn't want to tell me?' She held up the phone for Hunter when he strolled back in. He read Henry's alerts about Mike's girlfriend undergoing an emergency Caesarean after being rushed to the hospital and the colour seeped from his face. 'Partly.' He scrutinised her closely. 'You didn't know she was pregnant?'

'No.' The strength of her reaction shocked her. It hurt like a vicious stab wound to the heart to discover her ex-husband had given his new girlfriend the baby she'd wanted so badly. A healthy, if small, little girl.

'If it helps you any he's not happy about it.'

'It really doesn't. In an ideal world every baby would be wanted, loved and cared for, although I'm not naive enough to believe that's the case. Mike's not soft and fuzzy when it comes to children . . . or anything else.'

'Kiki going into labour early might be partly my fault.' He shoved a hand through his loose curtain of hair. 'I kind of interfered and might've upset her.'

'You? How do you know her?' Laura listened to his story with disbelief. 'You did that for me?'

'Yeah, mainly.' Hunter's sky-blue eyes darkened. 'But also because he's a piece of scum with the scruples and morals of an alley cat. The other doctor involved should be raked over the coals too.'

'I'll report them both on Monday.' She flopped down on the nearest chair.

'Hold your horses, sweetheart. I'm not sure Kiki will corroborate the allegation. Could be tricky.'

'What about if I talk to her?' Laura's voice wobbled.

'Are you prepared for all the gossip if you do that?'

'As a medical professional how can I ignore this? And as a woman . . . ' Out of nowhere an image filled her head of a tiny wrinkled baby, swaddled in a soft blanket and wearing one of the pink-and-white striped hospital knitted hats with an oversized bow.

'I'm dumb.' Hunter clutched her tighter. 'It's the baby, isn't it?'

Nodding through her tears Laura's longing for a baby poured out.

'Let's talk about this when you're . . . ' He hesitated.

'Not hysterical?'

'Don't put words in my mouth. How about we go upstairs?'

She didn't challenge him. For now she'd take what he offered exactly as he'd done with her the other night.

Hunter tightened his arms around Laura as she stirred in her sleep.

'Do you want to talk now?' she whispered.

With her warm, pliable body pressed against him their chances of having a sensible, unemotional conversation were zero. She sat up and tugged on a soft pink flannel pyjama top, treating him to a wry smile.

'I'm sorry. Hearing about Mike's baby caught me unawares. I didn't mean to freak you out.' Laura pushed her tousled hair out of the way. 'Polly has always assumed I'm too wrapped up in my career to want a family.' The harsh edge to her laughter sliced through him. 'Mike made the same mistake.'

'Didn't you discuss whether or not you wanted children before the wedding?'

'Yes, but we agreed to wait.' She briefly closed her eyes and took a deep breath. 'He assumed that meant I didn't want them at all while I took it for granted he would change his mind at some point in the future. We should have been more honest but that was never our thing'

'I'd tell it like it is because I know I'd be a lousy father.'

'Why?'

The simplicity of the question caught him unawares.

'You're a good, kind, loving man. What more does a child need?'

'Brett would describe our father that way but I don't remember a time when the two of us weren't at loggerheads. I can't risk ruining my kid's life that way.'

'He obviously made mistakes with you and I suspect he regrets them every day. Has he reached out to you recently?'

A stiff invitation to Christmas dinner. Brief email updates when his mother was ill. Passing Hunter's name on to a friend interested in one of his custom-built log cabins. He rattled off the list and avoided Laura's eyes. 'I guess I wasn't as forthcoming as I could've been.'

'How will you live with yourself if

something happens to him before you get a chance to at least try to reconcile?' Her eyes glistened. 'No family is perfect but I never doubted my parents' love and they never doubted mine for them. Every day in my job I deal with people who have that choice taken away and regret is the ugliest word in the English language . . . I'm pretty sure it is in the American one too.'

'I'll think about it. All of it. Okay?'

'Sounds good to me.'

He risked a fleeting grin. 'What time is your wedding overhaul session anyway?'

'Overhaul? You make Polly and I sound like a couple of old cars in need of a tune up.' Laura glanced at the bedside clock. 'She'll be here to pick me up in an hour. I ought to shower and — '

' — What you 'ought' to do first is let me make love to you again.' Hunter pushed her back down on the bed. 'That'll put a glow on your face and make the spa's job much easier. You'll need less make-up to fool people you're not past your sell-by date yet.'

'I should smack you and toss you out of bed!'

'But you won't.' He'd take the temporary reprieve and run with it. When she challenged him again Hunter hoped he'd be prepared.

23

Polly stretched out in the hot tub and took another sip of champagne. 'Tell me this isn't more fun that mopping up yucky stuff at A&E?'

'Much more fun.' Despite her earlier misgivings Laura had thoroughly enjoyed being pampered. Would she have relished it more without thoughts of Hunter McQueen intruding at regular intervals? Definitely. But a person rarely got everything they wanted.

'Make-up and nails next and then it's time for our fancy afternoon tea.' A cloud flitted across her sister's face. 'Mum would have adored all this.'

The grief of missing their parents had been the proverbial elephant in the room through all the wedding preparations, and they'd only dared release it on a few occasions.

'She would positively swoon over Hunter,'

Polly declared. 'She always had a thing about Americans and would've dumped Dad in a heartbeat if Robert Redford ever came calling.'

All morning Laura had tiptoed around her sister's pointed questions but now the gloves were off.

'Don't lie and tell me it's a casual fling because you don't do those, and don't claim he's only staying longer to follow up on Danny Pearce either.'

The second glass of champagne loosened her tongue and Laura poured out the whole baby story all the way through to her bedtime confrontation with Hunter.

'That's pants.' Polly topped up their glasses. 'What are you going to do?'

'About Mike? Report him. Not out of revenge because I'm way past that but because it's the right thing to do.'

'Good. He deserves it.' Polly's decisiveness made her smile. 'I'm not stupid. I know you've never told me everything about your crappy marriage and now I hate myself for never realising you wanted children.'

'That's not your fault. I kept it all to myself because that's how I am.' Laura sighed out her frustration. 'But I don't want to be that way any longer.'

'Do you think one day you'll stop treating me as your baby sister and we can try to be equals?'

She nodded.

'And Hunter?'

'He promised to — '

' — think about it all. I know, but you need to be more proactive than that.' Polly sounded vehement. 'Offer to help him reach out to his family. If he gets to a better place with them, I'm sure the rest will fall into place.'

Tears misted her vision.

'Come on, that's enough serious stuff. Let's finish our miraculous transformations so we'll be irresistible to our men by the time we get home.' She grinned. 'Johnny will have to wait to show his appreciation because I'll be busy decorating the church after this.'

Polly's optimism swept her along and

for the first time Laura recognised how smart her younger sister really was.

★　★　★

Hunter dug the photo he'd carried around for the last twenty years out of his bag. The crumpled, out-of-focus shot showed a group of fifteen or so teenage boys gathered outside an imposing red brick building. He ran his index finger over Danny Pearce's shock of white-blond hair. What was the best way to contact him? They could hardly turn up on his doorstep, and a phone call struck him as equally abrupt. He surely wouldn't accept a Facebook friend request from people who'd made his young life a misery, which left the old-fashioned option of writing a letter. But what to say?

'I'm home. This is the best they could do.' Laura struck a model girl pose in the doorway, shimmying her hips in a fit-where-it-touched silk dress which was the enticing colour of warm caramel. 'Polly insisted on buying this for me at the spa boutique. She said I wasn't coming back here in my boring jeans and jumper.'

His long, slow whistle made her blush. 'Wow, I'd no idea they could work miracles. Worth every penny.'

'Throw in the silver dress and ankle-breaking heels tomorrow and I might as well be a Barbie doll.'

He made a playful grab for her and kissed away every scrap of Laura's glossy peach lipstick. 'I'll kick Ken to the curb.'

'Have you been checking up more about Danny?' She gestured to his computer with the screen still open at a website about the history of the now defunct Greystone Institution.

'Well yeah, but don't you have wedding stuff to do with Polly?'

Laura laughed. 'I'm banned from helping to decorate on the grounds that I apparently wouldn't know a winter wonderland from a hole in the ground.'

'Sounds like you've had a lucky escape.'

'Considering you told me that your

usual New Year's resolution is to stay single I certainly don't see you and wedding planning as a match made in heaven either.'

Her casual dismissal stung.

'Come on now, you aren't trying to tell me you've had a change of heart?'

'I'd hardly go that far . . . '

'But?'

If he told the flat-out truth she might throw him out again but he refused to lie. Laura rested a finger on his lips, her eyes wide with pleading.

'Wrong time. Okay? Show me what you've been working on.'

He should be grateful for the reprieve, so why did it suck?

★   ★   ★

It took every ounce of self-control to hold her nerve under Hunter's scrutiny.

Being Polly's bridesmaid next week is the closest I plan on getting to an altar again.

She'd meant every word, but now?

Maybe he wasn't the only one rethinking the subject.

'Sure.' Hunter's deep voice rumbled through her. 'If you've nothing better to do I'd be glad of your input.'

Looking at the screen together meant sitting close. Too close. Inhaling his familiar scent was bad enough but the press of his solid arm against hers and the shadow of stubble darkening his jaw where he hadn't shaved in a couple of days conspired to undo her resolve. Her fingers were within touching distance of his thick hair until he pulled out an elastic band and yanked it back in a rough ponytail.

'Damn stuff gets in the way.'

'Have you always had it long?'

A weary smile creased his face. 'Nah, I grew it to piss off my short-back-and-sides father and kinda got used to it, I guess.' Hunter's eyes brightened. 'Women either love it or hate it. Sorts things out real fast.' The huskiness of his voice hinted they were on dangerous ground because they both knew which category she fell into. 'I held onto this photograph taken at the centre. That's Danny, front row, right hand side with the light hair.' He rambled through the various ways he'd considered to get back in touch.

'I agree a letter is your best bet.'

'But what the hell do we say?' he almost shouted. 'Sorry we messed up your life, pal. How you doin' these days?'

'I'm used to giving people difficult news if you want my help?'

He pushed the laptop towards her. 'Have at it. Maybe together we can come up with somethin' not completely lame.'

'Let me have a try.' She frowned at the screen and started to type. 'How about that?'

Hunter scanned through the letter she'd put together. 'Awesome. You're a genius. Can I print it off here?'

'Handwrite it. Much more personal.'

Laura pushed the chair back. 'I'm going to get changed into some comfy clothes and scrub this junk off my face.'

'Whoa, not so fast.' He caught her by the door. 'I lean towards the natural look usually but . . . ' One hand traced the curve of her hip. 'We sure aren't wasting this.' Hunter explored further and a wicked smile lit up his face. 'Oh boy, you never mentioned these.'

'What?'

'Stockings.'

'They were Polly's idea.' Her argument that they were uncomfortable hadn't cut any ice.

'I think I love your sister.'

So do I, she thought.

'Remind me to thank her tomorrow.' Hunter's lingering kiss awakened every nerve in her body until they all screamed and vied to be touched first. 'You can thank her too.'

'What for?' Laura's flirtatious reply made his eyes darken.

'I'm about to show you.'

She struggled to recall why she was off men and weddings but failed when Hunter swept her into his arms and made for the stairs as fast as he could.

24

Hunter waved Laura off in a taxi to help Polly get ready for the wedding and hurried back upstairs to sort himself out. The 'Enforcer' had left strict instructions for him to be at the church no later than quarter to twelve. Because he hadn't intended to stay for the wedding the only half-decent clothes he'd brought with him were a pair of black cord trousers, a matching shirt and black leather hand-tooled boots. It had been a challenge to find a jacket in Plymouth that fit him but he'd tracked down something and worked his charm on the shop's seamstress to get it altered in record time.

Laura appreciated the touch of flamboyance his long hair gave him so for her sake he'd leave it loose today. Hunter finished dressing and checked his appearance in the mirror. *Yeah, blendin' in wouldn't happen in this.* When he walked outside the taxi driver's smirk told him all he needed to know. Thankfully the weather had done a complete turnaround and they were basking in what he suspected was a rare rain-free, sunny January day.

'Here you go, mate.' The driver laughed as they drew up outside the church. He nodded towards the other guests walking in, the women in hats and elegant dresses and all the men wearing traditional dark suits. 'Their invitations must've forgotten to mention it's fancy dress.'

His three-quarter length black silk coat with ornate silver embroidery, wide black leather belt with a massive silver belt buckle and narrow black tie with a diamond encrusted silver clasp would be par for the course in Nashville. Not so here. With a quiet smile he gave the driver a generous tip and levered himself out of the car.

'Mr McQueen?' The grinning usher checked out Hunter then his list.

'You're at the front.'

'I don't — '

' — Johnny got overruled by the women.' The man chuckled. 'You were supposed to be sitting on his side of the aisle but Laura claimed you instead.'

Hunter's embarrassment deepened.

'Follow me.'

Oh well, as the Brits say — in for a penny, in for a pound.

★   ★   ★

'You were right.' Laura peeped in through the heavy oak door, opened ready for the bride's entrance. Pale sunshine streamed in through the stained glass windows and brought out an intoxicating fragrance from the abundance of flowers decorating every corner of the ancient church. Her sister's vision of a winter wonderland had come to life exactly as planned and no destination wedding could have topped this.

'How could you ever have doubted me?' Polly's light tone didn't cover the underlying seriousness of the question.

'I don't know.' If she hugged her sister she'd crease the sleek white satin dress with its billowing medieval sleeves and never be forgiven. 'It won't happen again.'

'Of course it will. You can't switch off like that.' Polly laughed and clicked her fingers. 'But we're in a better place now and that's a good thing.'

Laura cleared her throat and plastered on a bright smile. 'Come on, let's go and put poor Johnny out of his misery.'

'Let's hope Hunter likes the new sparkly version of my sensible older sister.'

With her hair swept into a soft up-do and the addition of a delicate silver necklace and drop earrings she had to admit the dress looked tolerable. 'I'm sure he'll appreciate it later.' They'd already shared a laugh about his gratitude over the stockings.

The music started and Laura nodded at Polly, their thoughts running along the exact same path. She'd offered to escort her sister down the aisle or suggested their Uncle Arthur as an alternative but Polly insisted on walking alone. No one could take their father's rightful place. Her sister's smile returned as she stepped forward.

Laura's glance lighted on Hunter. It was hard not to notice him when he stood head and shoulders above everyone else. Her smile broadened at the sight of his distinctive jacket with glittering silver embroidery to match her dress. Knowing he'd chosen it in solidarity with her increased the growing depth of her feelings for him. For a second she almost slipped up and used the dreaded L word.

'Are you going to take my bouquet or not?' Polly hissed and she brought her attention back, but not after catching the hint of amusement curving Hunter's lips.

As the couple spoke their vows she gave up the effort to hold back tears and they trickled down her face, no doubt taking her carefully applied make-up with them. The certainty in Polly and Johnny's voices set off an unwelcome surge of envy. By her own wedding day she'd already been having doubts about Mike and should have listened to them instead of convincing herself it would all work out.

'You definitely outshine the bride.' Hunter's familiar scent announced his presence behind her as the photographer attempted to shuffle them all around to his satisfaction.

'It would be hard not to in this dress.' She dragged her gaze over him. 'Of course I can't live up to your unique choice of wedding attire. Did you bring that with you from Nashville?' It struck her as something an old time country music singer might have worn.

'Believe it or not, I found it here and not at a fancy dress store either. I tracked down a shop catering to the entertainment business.'

'It's entertaining all right.'

Hunter slipped his arm around her shoulder. 'Couldn't have you grabbing all the limelight.'

'You've certainly succeeded in snatching your share.' Laura brushed a kiss over his warm cheek. 'I appreciate your thoughtfulness.' More than a few curious glances came their way, and she suspected they'd be the cause of rampant speculation at the reception and maybe a touch of green-eyed jealousy from a certain Irish lady.

'It's my middle name.'

True, but there's a lot more to you than that and here isn't the right time or place to say so. Her expression must have conveyed her thoughts because his eyes darkened.

'Later.'

Her logical, professional side told her that the luscious warm tingle spreading through her body was nothing more than a state of responsiveness to sensory stimulation triggered by his husky whisper. Her heart told her that was rubbish.

'Smile for the camera.' Hunter nodded towards the photographer and shifted his hand around her waist. The discreet squeeze he sneaked in sent her smile off the charts.

★ ★ ★

He didn't give a damn what anyone else thought about his fashion sense, or lack of it, not when it made Laura this happy. Heck he'd stroll through the streets naked if . . . well, maybe he wouldn't go that far, but the thought was there.

Johnny slapped his shoulder. 'Nobody's going to mistake you for an uptight Brit in that get-up.'

'Yeah, well, I can't help if you're all boring as hell.' Hunter grinned. 'My lady likes it, and that's all that matters.' Laura's sharp glance and his old friend's obvious surprise made him consider retracting the words but it was too late now.

'Better go, my wife is getting impatient.' He smiled broadly. 'Sounds bloody amazing to say that.'

'I'm sure it does.' He received another sideways look from Laura who read his every thought and intention these days.

He'd grown out of his youthful wilfulness and led a very productive life now, so was it completely out of bounds to wonder if they might experience that same level of happiness one day? 'We'll see you at the reception.'

'Make sure the bridesmaid gets there safely.'

'Will do.' They only had to walk a few metres to a small hotel down the street making it not much of a challenge. Before Laura could launch into him for making assumptions that weren't his to make, Hunter swept her to him for a long kiss. 'Did I mention how damn beautiful you look today?'

'Smooth-talking charmer.'

'Don't forget the later thing I just promised.' He lowered his voice. 'Let's go enjoy ourselves, and we'll sort the rest when we're done bein' the life and soul of the party.'

'I don't do 'life and soul'. Ask anyone who knows me.'

'Hey, you're with me now. We'll do this together.' Laura didn't object when he kissed her again, in fact if she'd responded with any more enthusiasm he was pretty certain they'd never make it to any reception.

'Maybe you're right.' Her shy whisper made him really want to be.

25

Laura stared around the room, empty except for Hunter who sat with his boots propped up on the table, the gaudy coat and tie abandoned hours ago. They'd stayed until the last reluctant guests departed and the hotel had cleared everything away. Johnny and Polly were on the train to London for their morning flight to sunny Barbados which left them alone, finally.

'I'm thinkin' it's time for the dance I couldn't have with you earlier.' He levered himself off the folding chair.

'We did dance.'

'Not the way I wanted.' Hunter's eyes shone.

'The DJ's gone.'

'No worries.' With a few taps on his mobile the sultry strains of 'Slow Hand' by the Pointer Sisters filled the room.

'You came prepared.'

'I always try to.' She stepped into his open arms, unconsciously moulding her body to his. 'But you knock me off-kilter so I don't know if I'm comin' or goin'.'

They moved in sync to the slow, thudding beat and he undid the sparkly clips holding up her hair, sliding his fingers through to shake the curls loose around her bare shoulders.

'Damn, this wasn't the good idea I thought it was.'

'Why's that, hotshot?' Laura was fully aware of his overwrought body.

'Because if we don't call a halt now we're gonna get caught by the hotel owners in a compromising position.'

'Why, Mr McQueen. You shock me.'

'I doubt that, sweetheart.' His wry grin made her laugh. 'You know darn well what you're doin' to me. Let's get back to your place and continue this . . . conversation.'

'Funny sort of conversations you have in Tennessee.' She stroked down the front of his shirt. 'They don't seem to involve much in the way of talking.'

'I know we need that too.' His smile faltered.

'Shush. There'll be time enough in the morning.'

'The Enforcer has spoken.'

Laura responded with a lingering kiss, unwilling to let go of the magic Polly and Johnny's shining love had woven around the day.

★ ★ ★

Most habits creep up on a person and waking up with Laura's soft, curvy body wrapped around him was one that Hunter didn't intend to break anytime soon. Long term? He couldn't go there yet.

One day at a time. That's what he told the troubled youngsters he worked with. For twenty-four hours listen to your parents' point of view without automatically writing it off as a load of garbage. Really think about the effect your harmful behaviours are having.

Consider whether it's a good way to live. If it's not what help do you need to change?

Maybe he needed to take a dose of his own medicine.

'If I confess something first, will that make it easier?'

'Didn't realise you were awake.'

Laura wriggled around to face him. 'It was pretty obvious *you* were.' Her downward glance and hot pink cheeks amused him.

'I'm not gonna apologise for the fact you turn me on.'

'Did I ask you to?'

'Nope.' He dragged them into a kiss, ignoring her muffled protest that she hadn't brushed her teeth. Ignoring his body's strangled protest he stopped there. 'How about showers and breakfast before we do the talkin' bit? Don't know about you but I'm starved and yeah I'll do the cookin'.'

'I must admit I'm hungry. I was too busy to eat much at the reception and then last night . . . '

'I didn't give you much chance to eat. The peanuts and crisps we snacked on don't count as a balanced meal. You lay there and rest a bit longer while I shower 'cause if you join me it'll delay things.'

'Can't imagine why.' She fluttered her eyelashes and he couldn't help thinking how much he loved Laura's playful side, something she'd insisted at the beginning that she didn't even have.

'Yeah, right.' Hunter reluctantly got out and tugged the duvet back up to keep her warm. On the way to the bathroom she cracked a ribald remark about objectifying men's bodies and he playfully shook his bare backside. 'Objectify away.'

He kept his shower brief because if Laura discovered cold water when she came in that wouldn't go down well. Downstairs he surveyed the meagre contents of the fridge and made a mental note to go food shopping later. For a second he pulled up short. Was it wrong to assume he'd be hanging around a while longer? Rory Watkins, his assistant manager in the business, assured him only yesterday that he could easily cope until Hunter returned. He glanced at his phone as an incoming message popped in. Brett again. They rarely had any contact when he was home so why a third message from his brother in just over a week? A tug of guilt pulled at Hunter because he had ignored the first two so he reluctantly opened it up.

Dad needs to see you but won't ask so I'm doing it for him. Think about coming to visit when you get back.

He briefly felt sorry for his brother stuck in the middle, but reconciling with his father wasn't going to happen second-hand. Hunter refused to think about it anymore for now and returned to the task in hand.

Coffee was the priority and he saw to that first, watching the fragrant dark liquid drip into the glass pot with satisfaction. In the back of the freezer he dug out a packet of sausages set them on low in a pan to start frying then whipped up a bowl of scrambled eggs to cook when Laura came down-stairs and sliced four thick slices of bread to toast.

'That's better.' Laura pulled a comb through her damp hair as she wandered into the kitchen.

He couldn't lie. It was impossible to consider baggy dark green sweats and fluffy red reindeer slippers an improve-ment on her glorious naked self.

'Get your mind out of the gutter McQueen, and feed me.'

'Yes, ma'am. Coffee comin' up.' In the middle of pouring her a large mug Hunter stopped. 'Were your folks this way?'

'What do you mean?'

'Havin' fun together. Jokin' around?'

★ ★ ★

Laura blinked away a rush of tears. 'Yes. They weren't soppy and all over each other but clearly enjoyed each other's company, and even when things were tough could always make each other laugh.' She swallowed hard. 'That's precious. I never shared that with Mike and before you ask I don't know why I settled for less than I . . . deserved. He's a brilliant surgeon and can be very charismatic when he puts his mind to it. I think because I initially showed no interest that's why he pursued me, but as soon as we were a couple he criticised everything from my weight to how close I was to my sister. Within months of being married he started to look elsewhere. That didn't do much for my self-confidence until I concluded the problem rested with him not me, which was when I left. What were *your* parents like?' Hunter's tight expression indicated he wasn't happy with her question but he'd started this conversation in the first place.

'I remember them being okay when I was a kid but later there was always an atmosphere.' He shrugged. 'I guess it was constantly hanging over their heads when the school would call about another problem I'd caused, or when the police might turn up on their doorstep. That might have made it kind of hard to laugh much. It didn't help things that they disagreed how to deal with me too.' Hunter rubbed at his temple. 'Mom even left once but only stayed gone a few weeks. That's when Dad took the job in London. Fresh start for us all.' The attempt to smile only made a slight curl in his top lip. 'I guess in the long run it did help me, but it was pretty brutal at the time. I'm pretty sure my folks are alright now but I live about four hours away from them and don't visit often. They don't seem to mind that any more than I do.'

She wasn't sure how to go about helping him to make peace with his family but felt in her gut he'd never really be in a totally good place until that happened. 'Do you think your brother might be willing to act as a sort of go-between?'

He drank his coffee and played for time by refilling their mugs. 'You're a good person, Laura — '

' — But it's not my business and I should shut up?'

'Don't put words in my mouth. I would never speak to you that way.' Hunter's protest made her guilty. She must stop assuming all men, and especially this one who'd been nothing but kind and loving towards her, resembled Mike. 'I was trying to say I appreciate your efforts to help and one day I'll think about taking your advice, but right now I've other things on my mind.'

'Danny Pearce?'

'Well yeah, that too. I was thinkin' more along the lines of . . . ' Leaning across he cupped her chin with his hand and drew them into a long, hot kiss.

'What about breakfast?' Laura croaked.

'I suppose I'd better feed you first or you won't have the energy for what I've got in mind.'

She recognised the stalling tactic but was learning that he didn't do well being steered towards something until he'd been given the opportunity to make up his own mind. Something she felt his father had never understood. 'And three guesses what that is.'

'You've got a dirty mind. It's another pretty day, and I thought we might enjoy a hike across the moors.' Hunter's eyes sparkled. 'After our walk is another story.'

'Thought it might be.'

'I'm gonna finish fixin' our food.' He raised one thick brow. 'Think you can babysit the toast while I see to the eggs?'

'That might not be too big a strain on my culinary skills.'

Hunter's phone buzzed and he frowned at the screen. 'It's from an unknown number in Newquay. Do you think it could possibly be Danny? He must have got my letter by now and I did include all my contact details. What do I do?'

'Answer it? It might not be him. Could be a double glazing salesman.'

With a grim expression, he swiped right to accept the call and turned on the speaker so she could hear the conversation.

224

'Hello, Hunter? This is Daniel. Daniel Pearce.'

Laura's heart thundered in her ears so she could only imagine what his was doing.

26

The deep voice retained the slight hesitance of the shy teenager Hunter remembered.

'Your letter took me by surprise.'

'Yeah, I suppose it — '

' — My first thought was that you've got a bloody nerve after all these years.' Danny steamrollered his attempt to explain. 'My second was to come to Plymouth and beat the living daylights out of you.' A mirthless laugh trickled down the phone. 'That would only work if I'd spent every day of the last twenty years in the gym and you'd shrunk.'

'Can't help you out there. I've filled out more and grown a couple of inches.'

'Right, I'll abandon that plan then.'

'Was there a third option?'

'My wife suggested inviting you here for lunch today, if you're free.'

The idea scared him shitless, but how

could he refuse? Laura pointed to herself and mimicked driving the car. 'That would be great.' *Liar.* 'Is it a problem if my . . . ' *Hell, what did he call her?* ' . . . my, um, girlfriend brings me? She doesn't have to stay.'

'Of course she can stay. We'll be delighted to meet her.' Danny rattled off directions to his house. 'It's a straight run down to Newquay and this time of year should only take you an hour or so. Plan to arrive about one.'

A moment later he was left holding a dead phone and wondering what he'd stupidly agreed to.

'Girlfriend?'

'Sorry, didn't mean to — '

' — Don't apologise! I like it.' Her face could do double duty as a traffic light. 'Anyone would think I was fifteen. Can people even be boyfriend and girlfriend when they're both well over thirty?'

'We can be whatever we want.' Hunter stroked a rogue curl back from her face. 'You're okay with the whole

lunch thing? I really need you with me.'
He couldn't remember the last time he
admitted that he needed another person.
Maybe that was one way he'd gone adrift
with his parents?

'I'm totally good with the whole
thing.' Laura snuggled into him. 'Those
sausages must be well and truly dead by
now. I hope you'll do better than this
the next time you promise to feed me.'

'Sit down and save your skills for
navigating y'all's weird roads and those
circle things.'

'I'll teach you to cope with round-
abouts yet.'

The promise of something longer
term between them hung in the air.

★ ★ ★

Laura's stomach rumbled as she merged
onto the A30 at Bodmin. 'I hope Mrs
Pearce is a good cook.' In the end neither of them had managed to do anything
more than push breakfast around the
plate.

'Me too. I have no idea what to expect.'

'We should be there in about another half hour.' Her promise did nothing to soften Hunter's strained expression. Laura gave up any further attempt at conversation until she turned onto Trelyn Road. 'If it was August it would've taken us twice as long because the roads would be jammed with cars and caravans trying to reach the beaches in Newquay.'

'Twice as long would've worked fine for me.' Hunter dredged up a half-hearted grin. 'Sorry, I'm bein' a jerk.'

'No. You're anxious and worried but not a jerk. There's number sixteen on the gatepost. This must be it.' She drove slowly down a long gravel drive lined with manicured yew trees and gasped when a stunning Georgian-style manor house appeared around the last corner. Even in winter the elaborate garden was brightened by a swathe of early daffodils and edged with massive deep pink rhododendron bushes in full flower. 'Wow, what a fab place.'

'Doesn't mean he's had a good life.'

Laura held her tongue. 'Let's do this.' She jumped out of the car first because otherwise he might sit there all day and, as they approached the glossy, black front door, a slender man in crisp chinos and a starched white shirt stepped out to greet them. Judging by his teenage picture, his white-blond hair was darker and thinning on top, but the pale blue eyes and thin mouth hadn't changed.

'Welcome to Newquay, Ms . . . ?'

'Williams, Laura Williams.'

He turned towards Hunter but his blank expression gave nothing away. 'Long time no see.'

'Daniel, whatever are you thinking? Bring our guests inside.' An elegant brunette appeared carrying a golden-haired baby girl and her smart dark orange dress and soft tan leather ankle boots made Laura feel her grey wool skirt and navy jumper looked mundane. 'I'm Eleanor and this little monster is Amy.' Her friendly manner smoothed over the lingering awkwardness hanging around them all.

Soon they were settled in a sunny living room, drinking martinis and admiring the incredible view. It was hard to overestimate the positive effect of a laughing eight-month-old crawling around the floor and Laura allowed herself to relax a little as the two men exchanged polite conversation about the weather.

'We can have a proper chat when Amy goes down for her nap but lunch is ready, so let's go ahead and eat. I hope you like roast beef and everything that goes with it?'

'I sure do.' Hunter's swift response made her smile. 'I could eat those Yorkshire pudding things by the bucket load.'

Eleanor grinned. 'I made plenty. Amy's enjoyed gumming on one already.'

'Is there anything I can do to help?' Laura offered.

'Word of warning, layin' the table's about her limit.' Hunter chuckled. 'Or carrying in dishes.'

'What a cheek.' She smacked his arm and everyone laughed. Laura had no problem being made fun of if it helped to break the ice.

Although she had been starving on the way down here until the food appeared she'd wondered if she would be too nervous to force anything down. Luckily it was all so delicious she had no trouble. Danny stayed quiet throughout the meal but she suspected he often left the talking to his gregarious wife. By the time a huge bowl of black cherry trifle appeared, little Amy was half-asleep in her highchair.

'Why don't you all go back to the lounge and I'll bring coffee in when I've got her down?'

The knife-edge tension returned and Laura slipped her hand into Hunter's, earning her a grateful smile. Now came the hard part.

* * *

'Danny, there's a question I've wanted the answer to for twenty years.' The words poured out of Hunter in a long breath. 'Did I — '

' — *You* want? You don't get to ask anything until I've had my say.' His voice rose. 'For a start no one calls me Danny any more. I returned to using my full first name the day I left that godforsaken place.'

'Sure, no problem.' He back-peddled, desperate not to make things worse.

'I didn't invite you here today to make you feel better.'

'Why don't you explain why you *did* want to see Hunter?' Laura's used the same quiet, firm tone she reserved for difficult patients.

'I hoped I might finally be able to put that part of my life to rest.'

'We're on the same page there. I need the same thing.'

'What do you want Hunter to tell you, sweetheart?' Eleanor joined them again and perched on the arm of Danny's chair.

'Why you turned on me that last day? Before then you always stuck up for me and anyone else who got bullied.'

'They'd finally worn me down,' Hunter admitted. 'I'd been at Greystone almost two years and because of my ingrained stubbornness it was a non-stop battle. I couldn't do it any longer. I'm sorry.'

'But didn't you also want to thank him?' Eleanor murmured.

'Thank me?' Hunter couldn't hide his incredulity. 'What for?'

'That day was a turning point for me, because I realised I couldn't rely on any-one except myself.' Danny grimaced. 'I half-hoped you'd stop me leaving because I had no plan and no clue where I was going.'

'Was it tough?'

'No worse than staying in that bloody dump a minute longer.' He shook his head. 'If I'd gone home to my aunt and uncle they'd have kicked me right back to Greystone. I made my way to Llandudno because I'd been there with my parents on holiday and . . . I took the good memories as a sign.' A rash of heat crept up his neck. 'I picked up work in a hotel kitchen and got room and board with the job.'

'But you were only sixteen. Didn't they need identification for taxes and that kind of thing?'

'No. A lot of those jobs are under the radar. They don't ask and you don't volunteer.'

'It's where he got his start in the hospitality business.' Eleanor's pride was unmistakeable. 'He owns a string of restaurants across the country now. Have you heard of Granite Grills?'

'That's you?' Laura piped up. 'Oh, the name. That's very clever.'

'Bit of a play on words.' Danny shrugged.

'Why?' Hunter couldn't get his head around it. 'Why would you want the constant reminder?'

The added years etched deep tracks into Danny's face. 'Because I don't ever intend to forget what I went through and what I've achieved since those days.' He clutched his wife's hand. 'If it hadn't been for Eleanor and now my daughter, I'd be a bitter man. Extremely rich but bitter and that's no way to live.'

'What about you Hunter? How has life treated you since your time at Greystone?'

Eleanor's question took him aback. He determined not to come across as self-pitying in front of this man who'd suffered so much.

The ear-piercing wail of an unhappy little girl streamed through the baby monitor and on the video feed they spotted her red-faced, kicking her legs like crazy and flailing her arms in the air to be rescued from her crib.

'Never any rest for weary parents.' Eleanor laughed.

'Do you mind if I come with you?' Laura jumped up from the sofa and Hunter stifled the urge to pull her back down with him. 'Be honest,' she whispered. 'That's all he needs.' Her gentle encouragement helped calm his nerves. This trip to England wasn't turning out anything like he'd expected.

27

'Life's been a bit of a mixed bag.' Hunter launched into everything that'd happened since they last met, leaving nothing out.

'I admire the work you're doing with young people.'

'You could consider a similar project here.' He didn't push, aware that everyone dealt with the past their own way.

'I'll definitely think about it.' Danny walked over to a dark slate-topped bar in the corner of the room and poured them both a generous measure of whisky. 'I think we deserve this. Don't know about you, but baring my soul doesn't come naturally.'

'It sure doesn't.' He savoured the welcoming burn in his throat.

'There's a lot of work being done here in reclaimed building materials these days. Not as much in the way of wood as you're used to but you strike me as adaptable. A man like you could make a killing.'

'And I'd want to do that because?'

'Eleanor straightened me out and, from the little I've seen of her, Laura could do the same for you.' Danny gripped his shoulder. 'Don't let her get away.'

He could claim that things were complicated but they were for everyone. Things hadn't been smooth sailing for Polly and Johnny and now they were on their honeymoon so perhaps he should listen and learn.

'Change of subject. What's Johnny Matthews up to these days? Apart from getting married that is.'

Safer topic. Hunter rattled off a brief synopsis of Johnny's life since they were at school together. 'It might not be my place to say but he carries a lot of guilt over taking part in harassing you back in the day.' He didn't mention Johnny's attempt to hide the past from his new bride.

'I considered taking all this to the police at one point and if it was only targeting the staff members who turned a blind eye I'd do it tomorrow, but I got to thinking about all the boys . . . and we were only boys at the end of the day. They've either made their peace or not with what went on and all our lives have been affected.'

They fell silent with the only sound coming from the gentle ticking of an antique grandfather clock on one side of the brick fireplace.

'To a large extent my time at Greystone made me the man I am today.' Danny wandered over to gaze out of the large bay window. The wind was picking up and white tips frothed the waves crashing against the jagged cliffs.

'Yeah, me too. My folks tried everything to put me straight but nothin' worked. Maybe I needed that place and everything it stood for to see where my life was headed.' He cracked a half-smile. 'I'd rather not have gone through it but we don't always get to pick and choose.' The nugget of sympathy he'd begun to feel for his parents grew with every passing day. Laura was right. Until he faced his family and they were totally honest with each other his attempts to move on would only ever be on the surface. 'When Johnny comes back from honeymoon why don't you come up to Plymouth and we can — '

' — have a drink for old times' sake? I don't think so.' Danny shook his head. 'Seeing you again has done it for me. I'm happy to lay things to rest now.'

A pang of disappointment shot through him, but Hunter realised it was more for himself and how he'd hoped this might play out. He suspected Johnny would be inwardly relieved while putting on a show of being disappointed with the outcome. 'Fair enough.'

'This little girl wants her daddy.' Eleanor sailed back in and deposited her daughter in Danny's arms.

For a second Hunter caught Laura's sadness as her gaze lingered on the gurgling baby.

'Do you fancy a stroll along the beach? We usually like to walk off a big lunch.'

'Thanks, but we'd better be gettin' back to Plymouth.' He sensed Laura's relief. 'Some poor nurse has to work tomorrow.'

The women took little Amy outside, leaving the two men standing together by the door.

'Thanks for getting in touch. It took guts,' Danny ventured.

'I don't know about that but thank you for . . . everything.'

'Are you ready?' Laura asked.

'Yeah, I'm ready.' He nodded at Danny. 'Definitely ready.' They both knew he meant far more than simply being all set to wedge himself in the tiny car for the drive back to Devon.

★ ★ ★

'Do you mind if I have an early night?' They'd been polite with each other since leaving Newquay. Hunter hadn't offered up any details about the chat he'd with Danny and she'd avoided mentioning little Amy.

'I take it that isn't a 'we'?' Hunter threw her a quizzical look. 'I'll move back into the guest room if you need space.'

This was the problem when people weren't honest with each other. A streak of irritation raced through her. 'This is stupid.' She folded her arms. 'We're talking.' A flare of admiration brightened his sombre gaze. 'Let's sit down and you can start first.' She ignored Hunter's raised eyebrows which seemed to say 'why me?'. 'Start with every detail of your conversation with Daniel including how it made you feel. It won't kill you.' Laura swallowed the lump in her throat. 'I'll do the same about Amy when you're through.'

'Fine.'

She suspected Marie Antoinette sounded more enthusiastic on her way to the guillotine. The only help she gave Hunter was by not interrupting or asking any questions until he slumped back in the chair.

'When somethin' has been hangin' over your head for two decades it's mighty strange to finally have the burden lifted.'

'In a good way?'

'Yeah, but the next task is tackling my family.'

'I'll do anything I can to help.'

'Including coming to Nashville with me?'

'Of course.'

'Seriously?'

'Unless you've changed your mind in the last two seconds?'

'No way,' he said quickly.

'Good, that's settled.' Laura twisted the corners of a paper napkin around her fingers, reducing it to shreds in the ensuing silence.

'Little Amy's a sweetheart.'

His kind tone unravelled her, and silent tears trickled down her cheeks. 'Yes.' Remembering the baby's hot hands clutched around her neck when she lifted her from the crib increased her sobs. 'It's ridiculous. I know it is. I'm not *that* old and — ' she gulped, ' — not having kids isn't the end of the world. I truly love my job and have a full life.'

'You tryin' to convince me or you?' Hunter's loose hair fell around his face and she couldn't resist stroking it away.

'Me, you old devil.'

'Hey, less of the old. Neither of us is past it yet'

'What you're telling me is to take a deep breath and stop panicking.'

'I don't have a death wish.' He toyed with her fingers. 'Nashville sure is pretty in springtime.'

'I could probably take time off in late April?'

'Perfect.' The single, soft word of agreement was all she needed.

'I've changed my mind.' His expression turned to stone and she could have kicked herself for speaking too fast. 'I mean about the nonsense earlier about having an early night on my own.' Laura pressed a hard kiss on Hunter's mouth and teased her fingers through his thick hair. 'In case I'm not being plain enough, I want you in my bed tonight.'

'Oh you're comin' across loud and clear. An early night sounds pretty appealing right about now.'

Another thought slipped back in, one she had pushed aside during all of the wedding fuss and today's trip to Cornwall.

'You're not doin' the mind changin' thing again I hope?'

'Definitely not.' Laura rushed to reassure him. 'I remembered about Mike, that's all. I need to talk to Kiki first before deciding anything else, don't I?'

'I reckon it'd be wise.'

'And we know I'm always wise.' Pulling him to her she focused every ounce of attention on him. 'Tonight's all about us.'

'You won't find any argument from me on that score.'

'Us' was an incredible word she never thought she'd enjoy using again that way.

28

Henry's concern lingered in his dark eyes. 'Are you sure you're up for this?'

'Seeing Ms Alford or getting Mike in trouble?' Laura fought to steady her voice.

'Either. Both.'

The hospital gossip machine would love all this but she suspected most people would be on her side. Mike was a brilliant surgeon but he'd sailed close to the wind on more than one occasion. After a patient complained about his rudeness following her surgery he'd received an official reprimand, but Laura was also aware of a couple of unofficial warnings given through the old-boy network.

'Let's get this over with and I'll go from there.' She tugged her ponytail tighter and straightened her tunic. After she took Henry into her confidence he'd offered to act as a go-between.

Kiki was still in the hospital recovering, and he'd only managed to persuade the young woman to see her by promising to remain in the room during their meeting.

The sight of the fragile new mother propped up in the bed touched Laura. Kiki's lank blonde hair hung around her thin face and made her huge blue eyes appear almost child-like. Barely stopping to say hello she was drawn to the plastic bassinette in the corner of the room as if by an invisible thread.

'She looks like her father.'

The young woman's defensive tone saddened Laura. She wasn't the one disputing Mike's parentage of the tiny baby girl, swaddled in a pink blanket and with a tuft of dark hair sticking out from under her soft knitted cap. 'Yes, she does.' Touching the baby's soft cheek would cross an unbreakable line and she plastered her hands to her sides.

Kiki nodded at Henry. 'This doctor says you want to get my Mike in trouble.'

Laura couldn't lie. 'I might, but I'm

not doing this for personal reasons.' She'd talked the whole thing through with Hunter for half the night until convincing herself she wasn't acting out of revenge. That time had long since gone. 'I'm sure Doctor Adebayo explained that it could be considered misconduct and not good medical practise for Mike to coerce you into having certain tests that might've endangered your baby.'

'I never said that, or if I did I didn't mean it. That American man got me all confused.' A mutinous expression settled around her thin lips. It would be hers and Hunter's word against this vulnerable woman and, taking into account Laura's personal history with both men, what was the chance they'd be believed? She'd ruin her own career for nothing.

Henry cleared his throat. 'Ms Alford, would you mind if we had a quiet word with Mike and the other doctor involved to make them aware of our concern without any formal complaint being made?'

She read in his eyes a plea for her to

248

go along with this as the best they could hope for.

'I suppose that would be all right.'

The distinctive wail of a hungry newborn filled the room.

'Can you pass her over to me? I'm not allowed to pick her up on my own because of my stitches.'

Laura stared in panic at the screaming, red-faced baby but Henry made no move to rescue her from this impossible situation. Gingerly she scooped up the infant and instantly the baby fell quiet and stared up at Laura. If she hadn't known it was impossible in a three-day-old baby she'd swear the little girl was smiling.

'Are you going to give her here or what?'

'Oh, yes sorry.' She lowered the baby into its mother's arms. 'We'll leave you to feed her in peace.' Laura touched Kiki's shoulder. 'I hope Mike treats you well and is a good father to . . . ' She hadn't heard any name mentioned yet.

'Demelza. Like the red-haired actress in that Poldark thing.'

'That's a lovely name.' She bit back a scream. Once she stupidly admitted to Mike that if she ever had a daughter she'd name her Demelza. All he did was scoff and remind her they'd agreed to not have children so if they ever 'slipped up' she'd better 'sort it out'.

Somehow she made it outside of the room before slumping against the wall and Henry half-dragged her into the nearest waiting room.

'If it's okay with you, I'll have a word with Mike's boss and tell Perry Manning the whole story. It's best if he issues the warning and tries to ensure Mike doesn't hang that girl out to dry.' He patted her hand. 'I know it's not the result you wanted but . . .'

'It's the best we can do. I only hope he trips up at some point and it won't get swept under the rug again.' Laura shrugged. 'I've been doing a lot of thinking recently and pretty much come to the conclusion I don't want to work here any longer.'

'You can't let him drive you away.'

Henry's panicked protest made her smile. 'I won't bloody let him.'

'I'm not being *driven* anywhere. This is my choice. I need a fresh start. The divorce only got me halfway.' Laura waved her hand in the air. 'There's a big world out there. Nothing says I've got to stay in this little piece of it.'

Henry cracked a toothy grin. 'It's the Yank, isn't it?'

'Yes, and no.' Hunter was the catalyst, but she'd been inching in this direction before he ever set foot in Plymouth. 'I'm starting off by taking a holiday to see him in Tennessee.'

'You sly old thing. You'll be up the aisle again and knee deep in kids before you know it.'

'How did you . . . ?'

'Know you want a family? I guessed years ago. Anyone who sees you around babies and children would have to be blind not to recognise it.'

'Polly didn't.'

'I bet Mr McQueen didn't need it spelling out.'

For the first time she held back from being completely honest with Henry. Some things were too personal.

'When are you going to resign?'

Laura appreciated the fact he didn't attempt to change her mind. 'Probably before I go on holiday.' She rolled her eyes. 'If I do it now everyone will assume it's because of Kiki and the baby. I've got some pride.'

'You're an incredible woman. I often wish . . . ' Henry couldn't meet her eyes.

'What?'

'Nothing.' His firm tone warned her not to ask again.

'I need to get back to work.' Laura brushed a friendly kiss on his cheek and could have sworn a blush heated his dark skin. She'd respect his privacy the same as he'd done for her over and over again. Her mobile buzzed with an incoming text and the sight of Hunter's name made her smile.

'You'd better catch up with lover boy before he frets over you all day.' Henry's booming laughter didn't embarrass her, because she didn't care any longer who knew of her feelings for Hunter McQueen.

★ ★ ★

'What have I done to deserve this?' Laura sniffed appreciatively at the steaming roast chicken dinner set out on her candlelit dining table. He'd filled a yellow plastic bucket with ice and turned it into a makeshift chiller for an expensive bottle of champagne. Hunter watched her good humour fade as she put everything together. 'Oh you've booked your ticket back to America, haven't you?'

They didn't do lies these days. When she returned from work he'd shared her frustration over Kiki's refusal to publicly condemn Mike but in the end agreed there was nothing more to be done. Her ex-husband's arrogance would trip him up soon enough. When she told him about her conversation with Henry he squashed a fleeting moment of jealousy, never wanting to head down the possessive route where she was concerned.

'Yeah. I'm sorry.'

'When?'

'Saturday. I would've delayed until Sunday so I could tell Johnny about Daniel face to face, but it would've cost a lot extra, and work's pilin' up back home. Rory's doin' a great job but I can't expect him to carry me any longer.' Laura buried her head in his chest. 'While you're working over the next few days I've got meetings set up with a few builders doing reclamation work here in the south-west.'

'Why?'

'I thought I'd check out Daniel's idea.'

'Maybe I'll fall in love with Tennessee.' A slash of heat warmed her cheeks. 'Oh, are we . . . ?'

'Goin' too fast?' Hunter grinned. 'At our advanced ages we can't afford to waste too much time.'

'You keep telling me we're not past it yet.'

He stifled her protest with a lingering

kiss. 'I'm teasing you. I thought you got my sense of humour these days? Tell me we don't have to go back to the white flag wavin' thing again?' He pointed to the food cooling on the table. 'Let's dig in while it's still fit to eat.' Hunter nuzzled her neck. 'I wanna make the most of every minute.'

'You're right. Pour me a drink and feed me then we'll discuss dates for my trip.'

'Yes, ma'am.' Nothing was going to spoil his last few days here. Reality would intrude soon enough.

29

'Wow, you've had quite a week and here was me thinking I'd be the one with the best stories to tell.' Polly raised her glass to Laura. 'When my sister decides to do something she doesn't waste any time. I thought you'd stay at Derriford until they gave you a gold retirement watch.'

Everything burst out of her the minute the happy couple walked through the door. After saying a tearful goodbye to Hunter at the bus station yesterday she'd wallowed in misery for a few hours before giving herself a stiff talking to.

'Would you mind very much if I moved . . . to wherever it might be?'

'Mind?' Polly grasped her hand. 'I'd miss you like anything but seeing you this happy . . . it means the world to me.'

Laura's throat tightened.

'After that bastard messed you around I thought you'd never smile again, and now you're full of all these amazing plans and it's fab.'

'Uh, do I smell something burning?' Johnny frowned.

'Oh damn!' Laura raced into the kitchen and flung open the oven door. She fanned the smoke with a tea towel before grabbing the tray of cremated garlic bread and tossing it in the sink. Luckily the lasagne she'd attempted to reheat was still on the borderline between golden brown and burnt.

There'd been no question of attempting the traditional Sunday roast with her limited skills so Hunter suggested the three of them ate the leftovers from the dinner he'd cooked on Friday night.

Add a bag of salad and frozen garlic bread. You can't go wrong.

Plainly that had been wishful thinking on his part.

'Don't worry it's not as if we need the extra calories.' Johnny patted his stomach. 'We've spent the week eating non-stop ... at least when we weren't — '

' —TMI!' Laura declared. 'I'm a new fan of sharing more with those people I'm close to but some things are waaay too much, and the gory details of your honeymoon fit in that category.'

'I was talking about scuba diving and exploring the island.' His glittering eyes belied his words and two bright hot circles appeared on Polly's cheeks. 'How about I open the wine and you dish up? Then I want all the details on Danny Pearce. Hunter's email didn't go into specifics.'

'No problem.' Ten minutes later she regretted that assumption because from being ambivalent about contacting their old schoolmate in the first place Johnny did a complete turnaround.

'I need to see him whether he wants to or not, and don't bother trying to get around Polly either. She's with me on this.'

Laura sneaked a glance at her sister who only slipped her arm through Johnny's and didn't break a smile, making it clear where her priorities lay.

'You must do what you feel is right.' She conceded. 'Do you want his phone number?'

'No, we'll drive down there tomorrow. Neither of us has to go back to work for a couple more days and if I turn up on the doorstep he can't avoid seeing me.'

'You might not find him at home. He told us he travels a lot checking up on his various restaurants and usually takes his family with him.'

'I'll take the chance. If I need to I'll go back again and again until I catch him there.'

'Well good luck. You'll have to let me know how you get on.' She sipped her wine. 'I want to hear what you think of my revamped house.' In between visits to builders Hunter had spent every spare hour of the last few days wielding a paint-brush. Now she was the proud owner of a cheerful blue kitchen, a stylish lilac bedroom and a pale green bathroom complete with a newly installed electric shower they'd had great fun testing out.

She gulped down an unexpected rush of emotion.

'You miss him, don't you?' Polly's sympathy made it worse and poor Johnny looked as though he wished he could vaporise. 'Tell me about your holiday plans.'

Talking about her upcoming trip helped and she calmed down. 'Thanks, little sister.' She managed a feeble smile. 'I know I'm not supposed to call you that any longer but I can't help it, and it doesn't mean I value your help and opinions any less.'

'That's all that matters.'

She couldn't say any more and stared down at the untouched food on her plate before scooping a forkful of lasagne. 'Eat up. The chef wants a report later.'

★ ★ ★

It didn't matter whether he was studying a new cabin design, paying outstanding bills or catching up with the laundry all Hunter saw was Laura's pinched, white face on the day he left. The weather had unkindly recreated their first meeting with a brutal easterly wind and stinging rain but the major difference came in the heart-breaking way she clung to him instead of trying to wriggle out of his arms. They'd squeezed in as many hot, desperate kisses as possible before he was forced to climb on the bus.

To survive the next six weeks he needed to follow Laura's example and compartmentalise. She admitted once that the hard-learned ability to tuck away her emotions was one reason she was good at her job.

For my patients' sake and my own mental stability it needs to be that way.

Johnny's determination to visit Danny was another concern niggling away at him. He'd been to Cornwall twice already with no luck and intended to try again at the weekend. Hunter had briefly considered warning Danny but abandoned the idea because if Johnny ever found out he'd be furious. Not a good move for family harmony or his future with Laura.

Future with Laura. Some days those words sounded wonderful and on others more than a touch scary. Did she feel the same way? The supposed ease of long distance relationships these days was a fallacy in his opinion. How could anyone have deep and meaningful discussions on Skype or FaceTime?

Then there was his brother's letter to worry about. He almost missed seeing Brett's note in the middle of his pile of accumulated mail and came close to tossing it out with the pizza coupons and charity requests. Despite re-reading it multiple times Hunter still had no clue how to respond. A loud rap on the front door startled him, and he expected to see one of his neighbours or a lost delivery driver on the step.

'Oh hey, this is a surprise.'

'Is it?' Brett scoffed. 'Can't imagine why. You've ignored all my attempts to contact you so I've sacrificed my first free day in a month to come here.'

There were new lines etched in his brother's craggy face and streaks of grey woven through his close-cropped black hair.

Nothing like family guilt. 'Is not replying to one letter a capital crime now?'

'What about all the text messages I left on your mobile? I guess you were too busy having a good time to care what was goin' on with us.'

'I looked at the last one and all you said was Dad wanted to see me. He hasn't bothered much about me all these years so I assumed it could wait until I got back,' Hunter explained. 'I told you I was goin' to England for an old friend's wedding.'

'You said for one week, and it's been at least three now. Didn't it occur to you we might worry?'

Not really, he thought. 'Sorry. Come in.' He didn't have to wait long for Brett's lecture to begin.

'You'd better make whatever arrangements you need because you're coming back with me to Nashville now.'

'I can't!'

'You damn well can.' Brett's florid complexion darkened. 'Dad's having open heart surgery tomorrow. He won't beg you to come but he really wants to see you beforehand in case . . .'

How will you live with yourself if something happens to him before you get a chance to at least try to reconcile? Laura's warning slammed back into his brain.

'You didn't say anything about him being sick. A bit out of the blue, isn't it?'

'Not really. He's had problems for years with angina.'

'I didn't know.' The telling statement earned him a shrug. 'Maybe I should have but that's the way of it.'

'Does it need to be?'

'Maybe not.'

'He's gone downhill over the last few months,' Brett's voice turned husky. 'If this quadruple bypass isn't successful I reckon we'll be planning his funeral.'

The blunt assessment stunned him. 'I'll make a couple of calls and throw an overnight bag together.'

'Thanks. I promised Mom you'd come through.'

'She doubted me?'

Brett glanced away. 'Do you blame her?'

'No.' He honestly didn't but it still hurt. There was a lot he needed to share with his brother but four hours stuck in a car together allowed plenty of time to dump it all out.

30

'Come closer son, so I can see you better.' His father struggled to sit up. 'My nurse insists these damn dim lights are more calming for stressed out patients. Load of garbage.'

Still the same old man thinking he knew best. Hunter had struggled to hide his shock at Warren McQueen's deterioration in the six months since they last saw each other. The big-boned man had shrunk away to nothing and could barely speak without gasping for breath despite the oxygen tubes in his nose.

'I'm sorry for . . . ' His sorrow over his dad's health seemed irrelevant compared with everything else Hunter needed to apologise for.

'Let me talk first.' Warren nodded towards the door. 'The dragon won't let us have very long.'

'Is the nurse that bad?'

'The nurse?' His father attempted to smile. 'I'm talkin' about your sainted mama.'

Hunter couldn't speak. He realised that Laura would protect him in the same way.

'I'm mighty sorry for the mistakes we made raising you . . . no, the mistakes I made. Your mama didn't agree with my strict methods and I should've listened to her.' He visibly gathered his strength to keep going. 'Your brother's personality suited my way of doin' things but you were a different kettle of fish.' The edges of Warren's thin dry lips turned up. 'My bottom line was that if I said a thing was a certain way you needed to accept it without arguing, but you wanted explanations for every darn thing. If I said something was black you always insisted it was white.'

'I haven't changed. I'd have been lousy in the military because unquestioning obedience doesn't come naturally to me.'

'I know, son. I should've allowed for

the differences between you two boys but I'm a stubborn old cuss too.' A twinkle lit up his dull blue eyes. 'Maybe we're more alike than we realise.'

For once Hunter held his tongue and considered the possibility his father was right. Laura would call that progress.

'That damn school in England was my worst mistake.'

'Maybe not.' Hunter begged his father to be quiet for a few minutes. 'I need you to hear a few things.' Without going into details he skimmed over his time at Greystone and explained how he'd reconnected with Johnny and Danny. 'I'm not denyin' a lot of bad stuff went on but Danny claims it made him the man he is today, and I'm beginnin' to see it did the same for me.'

'Can you forgive me?'

'There's nothin' to forgive.' For the first time ever he meant it. 'We all make mistakes. I've made a shed load and my worst fault is holding onto grudges. I should've let it go and moved on.'

'Easier said than done.'

'Yeah, but it shouldn't have taken you . . . '

' . . . being on my deathbed to get us talking again?'

'You're not!'

'I am and we all know it. Even the doc says it's fifty-fifty whether I'll come through the op.'

Hunter's eyes burned.

'It's okay. If we're good now I'm at peace with whichever way it goes. Given a choice I don't want to leave y'all yet and especially the grandkids. I'm soft and let Caleb and Ava do anything they want. Ironic, isn't it?' His father's stare intensified. 'There's something else up with you, isn't there? I bet it's a good woman and about time too.'

With a sheepish grin plastered all over his face he talked about Laura. 'You'd better hang on a bit longer so you can meet her.'

'I'll do my best.'

You always did in your own way, he thought to himself.

They fell into a comfortable silence

until his mother arrived to shoo him out. Hunter calculated the time difference and decided to call Laura. Having someone special to share his worries with altered everything.

★   ★   ★

When Henry told her he'd seen a great last-minute deal to Nashville advertised he had asked what was stopping her going when Hunter clearly needed her there.

Thanks to his persistence Laura was now clutching onto the plane's armrests for dear life as they shuddered on their descent into Nashville. For the first time ever she'd thrown professionalism to the wind and begged for ten days off — promising to work all the unsociable hours going when she returned if her colleagues would cover for her. Right now she regretted not telling Hunter about her impetuous decision because she'd love nothing better than to see his handsome, smiling face in the arrivals hall. Hunter had sounded desperately alone when they spoke, and she was afraid the tentative bridge he'd built with his family wasn't strong enough to support him.

After all the landing formalities Laura should have been dead on her feet but years of shift work combined with almost overwhelming excitement at the prospect of seeing Hunter again brushed away any hint of tiredness. She thrust the scrap of paper with the hospital's information at the taxi driver and fell into the back seat to snatch a quick cat nap on the way. Years ago she trained herself to put sleep in the bank when the opportunity arose.

'Here you are, ma'am. Go in the main door and ask for directions at the hospitality desk. You'll want the fifth floor.'

Looking up at the towering skyscraper with its tinted windows and signs for valet parking she thought the driver had made a mistake and brought her to a fancy hotel instead of a hospital. 'Thanks.' That thought was confirmed as she entered the marble-tiled lobby, set off with plush leather couches, edgy artwork and massive potted plants. What would she do if Hunter had gone home for a break? Had he even mentioned her to his family?

'Laura? Am I hallucinating?' Hunter, grey-faced and strained, stared at her in disbelief. In seconds his massive arms tightened around her and his wonderful, woodsy scent brought tears to her eyes.

'I thought I'd surprise you.' She'd explain the full story later but for now nothing mattered except the joy in his deep blue eyes.

'My brother isn't the only surprised one.'

Another man's deep drawl startled Laura and she eased out of Hunter's grasp. The resemblance was obvious, although Brett McQueen was older, shorter and less muscular.

'You must be Ms Williams.'

'Laura, please.' They shook hands and she registered the smooth skin of a man who worked a desk instead of on the land. His pale blue hooded eyes were wary. 'I thought Hunter might appreciate — '

' — You don't have to explain yourself.' Brett's quiet statement put him firmly in her corner and a slash of heat coloured his hollow cheeks.

She couldn't believe she'd forgotten to ask after their father in all the confusion and her question drew a faint smile from both men.

'He's recovering well and back to ordering everyone around.' Hunter's reply implied amusement rather than animosity. 'They reckon on keeping him another couple of days before sendin' him home. We left Mama sittin' with him while we grabbed a late dinner.'

'Why don't I leave you two to chat and you can come up when you're ready?'

She smiled at Brett's offer. No doubt he wanted to give his parents advance warning of her arrival along with his first impressions.

'Nah, we'll go together.' Hunter grasped

273

her hand. 'You good?'

'Of course.'

Upstairs she realised they'd under-estimated Brett when a petite blonde flung open a door and beamed over at Hunter. Almost certainly this was who he'd been texting in the lift.

'You bring that little girl over to meet me right now.'

Martha McQueen struck Laura as younger than she expected but on closer examination she suspected a plastic surgeon of being involved in the mild deceit. She stifled a sneeze when Hunter's mother pulled her into a perfumed hug.

'So you're the cute little old Brit who's won my boy's heart.'

'Um, well . . .'

'She sure has, Mama.' Hunter's blatant declaration stunned her. 'If we don't take her in to see Dad right away he'll need more surgery. I'm sure he knows Laura is here too.' He gave Brett a long stare. 'Patience isn't his strong suit.'

She would have given anything for a

few minutes alone with Hunter because their scrappy emails and interrupted phone conversations had only given the barest insights into how things stood between the two men. But Laura was used to playing things by ear in her job and one difficult man wouldn't ruffle her.

31

Hunter watched his father fall under Laura's spell as they chatted about his surgery and loved how she turned it around when Warren quibbled about following his doctor's recovery plan.

'Don't you want to play with your grandchildren again as soon as possible?' Laura homed in on the one reason above all others that would get his father's attention.

'Yep.'

'Then this isn't the time to be stubborn except when it comes to pushing through the exercises you don't feel like doing and making sure you eat right.' She grinned. 'Be as stubborn as you like about those things.'

'You're quite a gal. I can see why my son's a changed man these days.'

He stiffened, unsure about the pointed comment until Laura treated him to

276

one of their private looks that told him to ignore it because she intended to.

'You need to rest as much as possible so we're going now.'

Hunter admired the way she didn't ask.

'We'll see you again in the morning.'

Outside the room she seized his hand with a brilliant smile. 'Hang on a minute.'

'Why?'

'You haven't kissed me yet.'

'I haven't had the — ' Pressed back against the wall with her fingers tangled in his hair he gave up his breath to her long, searching kiss. With a satisfied smile she wiped a smudge of pink lipstick from his mouth.

'That's better.'

'Sure is.'

'Was it really okay for me to turn up this way?'

A shadow flitted across her face and Hunter clasped her in a tight hug. 'More than okay. It was awesome. I needed you real bad.'

'Good.' Laura blushed. 'I don't mean

I'm pleased things are bad . . . oh you know what I mean at least I hope you do because — '

This time *he* silenced *her* with a lingering kiss. Smoothing back a lock of hair that had worked loose from her ponytail, he smiled. 'Everything's good and yeah I mean pretty much everything.' Hunter glanced around to make sure his mom and Brett weren't hovering within earshot. 'Let's get out of here.'

'I haven't booked anywhere to stay. Are there any hotels nearby?'

'Yeah, but you're comin' with me. I'm stayin' in Franklin at my folks' house. It's about a half hour drive from here and there's plenty of space in my bed for a certain delectable nurse.'

'I don't want to offend your parents.'

'Don't fret. For a start Mom and Brett are planning to stay here with my dad.' Hunter grinned. 'Plus, they know I've never been the conventional type and I'm not likely to start now.' He sensed a lingering reluctance in her silence. 'If it bothers you, we'll fix you

278

up in one of the spare bedrooms and I'll stick to . . . visiting you.'

'Would you mind?'

He cradled her face with his hands. 'I'll never mind makin' you happy whatever it takes.'

'You're a wonderful man.'

'Yeah, well, you're pretty darn good yourself.' Not the last word in eloquence but she didn't expect that from him.

'What the heck did you say to Dad?' Brett stormed out of the waiting room. 'He just ordered me to go home and take Mom with me. Claimed he'll get more rest without us hovering over him.'

Hunter fought back a smile. His father had taken Laura's advice seriously.

'That's my fault.' Laura reiterated her professional opinion.

'Fair enough, I suppose.' Brett conceded. 'The hospital can call us if there's any change in his condition. Will you take Mom on home with you, bro?' He checked his watch. 'If I get my skates on, I might catch the kids before they go to bed.'

'Yeah, no problem.' Talk about being foiled. There'd be no creeping around in the night sleeping next door to his insomniac mother. A brainwave struck him. 'I expect Laura will be messed up with jet-lag in the morning so why don't you collect Mom after breakfast and bring her back here? We'll visit Dad later in the day.' Hunter sensed Laura's amusement.

'Fine.' Brett fixed his gaze on Laura. 'I'll leave you to explain the plan to Mom. Good night.'

'Devious man.' Laura muttered as his brother hared off down the corridor. 'He is such a lawyer.'

They burst out laughing because what else was there to do?

⋆ ⋆ ⋆

She struggled to focus on the luminous red numbers and decided they were a nine and two zeros without any clue whether it was morning or night time. A few more brain cells stirred, helping her to decide that sunlight wouldn't be streaming in through the window this late in the evening in February.

'Are you awake? I've got breakfast for you,' Hunter called from outside the bedroom door.

'Come on in. You know I never turn down food.'

'Hope you won't turn me down either.' He sauntered in carrying a loaded tray.

'Is your mother around?'

'She's safely at the hospital driving my dad crazy again.' Setting down the tray he stripped off his T-shirt and sweatpants, pulled back the fluffy pink and white duvet and slipped in next to her. 'Do you want to eat first or . . . ?'

'Still the smooth charmer I see. I notice you left the other option to my imagination.'

'You've got a good one.'

Laura snuggled into him and ran her fingers down his warm, solid chest.

'Did I tell you last night how happy I am you came?'

'Yes, but I'm more than fine with letting you prove it right now.'

'Yes ma'am.'

Next thing she lay flat on her back with Hunter braced over her, settling himself in such a way as to leave his happiness in no doubt. A while later she decided sex was the best jet-lag cure ever.

'Oh Lord, you should come with a danger sign 'round your neck.' He rolled off her, gasping for breath.

'So, asking for more would be greedy and . . . possibly lethal?'

'Honey, I'll give it my best shot but — '

' — I'm teasing.' The flash of relief in his eyes made her giggle. 'You've turned my bones to jelly and I'm not sure I'll be able to move this side of Christmas.'

Hunter gently prodded her all over. 'Bones are still intact.' He slid a hand over her breast and the shivering sweep of his fingers made her skin tingle. 'On the other hand, I might've been a bit quick to reject your idea.'

She glanced downwards. 'I've created a monster. Sorry but you'll have to hold *that* thought until later. I'm starving.'

'Fair enough, I'll give you a break.' Hunter grimaced at the abandoned food. 'That's not fit to eat now. How about you have a shower while I fix a fresh round?'

'For safety's sake I'd recommend putting some clothes on before frying bacon.'

'Wow, that's a smart idea.' He smacked his head. 'Would never have occurred to me. I'm glad you're around to give me cookin' advice.' Hunter's smile turned evil. 'Burned any garlic bread and lasagne recently?'

'The lasagne wasn't — ' Laura's face heated. 'How did you know about that? Oh, don't tell me. No doubt my sweet sister took great pleasure in passing on that little gem.'

He threw back the covers, rested his hands behind his head and stretched like a satisfied cat. 'Maybe.'

'Get out of bed and down in the

kitchen before I die of starvation.' The jab she gave his ribs made him yelp. 'Don't you dare say that's not likely. Since you've been around, I'm learning to embrace my womanly figure.'

'Yeah, me too.' Hunter pounced and next thing they rolled off the bed onto the floor and breakfast was forgotten for the second time.

★ ★ ★

'So that's about it, honey. You were right.' Hunter topped up Laura's coffee mug. She'd intended to opt for tea until scrutinising his mother's meagre selection of herbal and decaffeinated tea bags and declaring there wasn't anything strong enough to face a long, jet-lagged day. 'Once Dad and I hashed things out there weren't any big sticking points between us, nothing important enough we couldn't let it go.'

'That's wonderful.'

'Brett actually listened for once when we were drivin' down here and didn't go all older brother on me.'

'Polly and I are working on that same issue too.' She scrutinised him. 'What is it? There's something you want to ask me, and you're putting it off.'

He was pretty sure Laura would have been condemned for witchcraft back in the day. Not that he'd any desire to keep secrets from her but hiding anything from this intuitive woman was damn near impossible. 'When we chatted the other night you told me the basics of what happened with Kiki, but I'm still not sure how you feel about it?' The sparkle he'd put in her eyes dimmed and Hunter touched his hand to her chin so she had no alternative but to look at him. 'It's okay to be ambivalent. Everythin' doesn't have to be black or white.' He cracked a smile. 'My dad's just comin' to that conclusion and he's nearly seventy so don't be too hard on yourself.'

'Ambivalent is a good word.' She sighed. 'I'm getting there, okay? I understand Kiki's reasoning but part of me wishes he'd been made to pay for his behaviour.'

'He will one day.'

'You can't be sure.' Laura frowned.

'No, but do you want to waste energy you could put into enjoying life or making a positive difference in the world into resenting Mike Russell for one more minute.' Hunter clasped her shoulders. 'He's taken enough from you, sweetheart don't let him have the last laugh.'

'My turn to say you're right, I suppose.'

'Yep, it sure is.' He hated to ask the next question but needed to know. 'How long do we have?'

'You don't mean today, do you?' When he didn't reply she sighed. 'A week. I couldn't get any more time off work.'

'I'm not complainin'. I'm still floored that you came in the first place.' Hunter twirled a loose end of her hair around his finger, playing for time.

'Say it.'

'If Dad gets out okay, in a day or two

286

how would you like to see my home?' His embarrassment deepened. 'We could take a run up to Knoxville and stay overnight.'

'I'd love that.'

'Really?'

'Yes, really.'

'It's not the prettiest time of year. Another couple of months and everything will be turning green and the spring flowers all comin' out. But it's still real special in that stark wintery way. A bit like your Dartmoor.'

Laura brushed a kiss on his hot cheek. 'You don't need to sell it to me.'

He knew he did because he was on the verge of asking something it was too soon for. Logically he should wait but seeing his father clinging to life a couple of days ago set him to thinking. Learning from the past was one thing but allowing it to define the present verged on criminal.

'Talk to me at your cabin. I've things to tell you too.'

God, she was so smart. He sure as

heck didn't deserve her but would fight to his last breath to secure her place in his life.

32

Laura did her best to be objective but instantly fell in love with Hunter's gorgeous cabin and its beautiful setting about a mile outside of Brush Creek, a community that hardly warranted the title of village with its small cluster of houses and single all-purpose shop. They ignored the chill in the air to eat lunch out on the porch, bundled up in thick jumpers and with cosy plaid blankets tucked around their legs. He'd designed it to wrap completely around the house and make the most of the views in every direction. Right now the only noise came from the birds chattering in the trees and her lover's soft snore as he dozed in one of the antique rocking chairs. She ran her fingers over the curved arms of her own rocker, the wood burnished by a combination of age and generations of stroking hands to a soft honeyed colour.

When they'd arrived Hunter had given her a quick tour of his home, and his passion for the place he'd created with his own hands was dazzling. He could recite the history behind every piece of wood, some salvaged from old barns and others saved from disused factories or shops. The comparisons with her cookie cutter house couldn't be more glaring.

There wasn't another home in sight, the gravel road would never have cars parallel parked 24/7 and the constant rumble of lorries along the main road wouldn't be a problem here, because they would find it a challenge to make it up the winding hilltop roads. She'd always considered herself a town girl who enjoyed the countryside without wanting to live there but this made her rethink everything. She'd declared her intention to resign from the hospital and assumed that she'd get another nursing job because being a nurse was an integral part of who she was . . . but maybe that was negotiable too?

When she tossed out the idea of moving to Polly, did this place nestle in the back of her mind even then?

'Winters can be a challenge.' Hunter stirred and stretched. 'Sometimes I sleep in my office in downtown Gatlinburg because the roads are too bad to make it back up here.'

'I can't imagine you living anywhere else.'

'I'm adaptable.' His eyes narrowed on her and she caught his hitched breath. 'At the end of the day unless you're around, I'll be damn miserable.'

'What are you saying?' A nervous wobble betrayed her conflicting emotions.

'The only obstacles are the ones we place there.'

'Obstacles to what?'

'Oh, Laura.' Hunter pushed up from the chair and straightened his back out before beckoning her over. 'Come here.' As he'd done so many other times, he didn't speak but simply held her. Before meeting him she'd never experienced the magical powers of a warm, all-encompassing hug and now was convinced its benefits should be available on the NHS. 'I need you to be part of my life. In fact, I can't imagine it without you these days.'

'But we haven't known each other long.'

' — do you see me down on one knee waving a diamond ring around?'

'Well, no.'

Hunter's kiss, laced with hints of the sweet apple pie they'd eaten, centred her on what genuinely mattered. He rocked gently against her core and it took all her resolve not to suggest they take the conversation back to the bedroom. With a rueful chuckle he held her at arm's length. 'I've got the willpower of a gnat around you.'

'I think that was a southern style compliment.'

'Sure was.'

'I said I had things to tell you, but you stole my line.' Hunter gave her a quizzical smile. 'Being unable to imagine my life without you was supposed to be my big declaration.'

'I've no objection to sharin' it.' He looked bashful. 'In fact, it's damn good to hear we're on the same page.'

For the first time she caught a glimpse of how the future might look if they had the courage to grab it.

*   *   *

Saying the right thing had never been his strong suit but thankfully Laura didn't expect Shakespearean wordiness from him.

'Forget about logistics.' Her smile encouraged him to touch her again, restricting it to grasping her small, sturdy hands in the hope that he could still use his head to think instead of less cerebral parts of the body. 'I reckon we can give the long distance thing a try while we explore our options.' Hunter held his breath, unsure if it was a good or bad sign when Laura's expression didn't change.

'That works for me.'

'Uh, good.' Shouldn't it be more momentous when two people reached an important crossroads and chose to go in the same direction?

'In case you weren't certain, I'm really, really happy right now.' Golden sparks set fire to her laughing eyes. 'You did all that perfectly.'

'I did?'

'Oh yes, only one thing would make it better.' Laura shook a warning finger in his face. 'I'm not talking about rings and proposals, silly man. Not yet.' Trailing a path down his chest she lingered on the zipper of his jeans. 'The king-sized bed you showed me earlier looked very . . . spacious.'

'Let's christen it.' A flare of surprise heated her pale skin. They hadn't discussed his past love life beyond the bare bones, so she wasn't to know he'd never brought another woman here. When he admitted the truth, she rewarded him with one of her glorious, verging-on-triumphant smiles.

And to think at one point he'd regretted accepting Polly's invitation to Plymouth.

Much later he checked his phone while watching Laura sleep. Most of his messages and emails were work related, all of which Rory could deal with until he returned to work next week. But one heading stood out and he clicked to open the attachment.

'Well I'll be damned.' Hunter peered at the photo a second time and Daniel and Johnny's smiling faces stared back at him.

'Wow that's . . . unexpected.' Laura wriggled in under his shoulder.

'You can say that again.'

Things were a bit dicey at first, but we talked things through and we're good now. You were right about me needing to face up to the past, although that makes your advice about staying away from Daniel flat out wrong. Ha ha! Can't win them all! Polly and I even got an invite to spend a week in Cornwall in the summer. Hope your dad's doing well and you and Laura are behaving yourselves — or not! J.

'If it's any consolation, I thought you

were right on both counts.'

He tossed the phone aside and wrapped his arms around Laura. 'Sure is, but I'm happy to be proved wrong. We've changed the way we cope with the fallout from the past — isn't that what learning from history is all about?'

'Very profound for a lazy afternoon.'

'Yeah, well that's me. Profound.' Hunter chuckled. 'Are you up for more exercise?'

'I thought I'd worn you out?'

'You've got a one-track mind.'

'I do?'

'Yeah, if you can drag your mind out of the gutter long enough, I was going to suggest a hike.' The blush spreading all over every inch of her smooth, pale skin almost changed his mind. 'I want to give you a taste of the Smoky Mountains so you can see how it compares to Dartmoor. I could take you to one of the popular tourist spots like Laurel Falls, but I reckon the area around here is equally pretty.' He tried to explain why it took him so long to pick the perfect spot for his cabin. 'I needed its fairly close proximity to Gatlinburg for work but couldn't stand living in the middle of all that hullabaloo. Pigeon Forge is even worse.' Hunter couldn't get through there fast enough these days past the tacky souvenir shops, unhealthy all-you-can-eat buffets and overpriced play areas designed to lure in gullible families. 'Gets me why people come to this area and spend a bomb on takin' kids to a dinosaur miniature golf course when you can take a picnic and hike in the mountains for free.'

'If you ever have dinosaur loving children you might change . . . ' Laura buried her face in his chest. 'Sorry.'

Hunter sighed. 'You have nothin' to be sorry for.'

'But — '

' — But nothin'.' He scooted down in the bed forcing them face to face. 'You've shaken my world, Laura. I'd come to the conclusion I was better off alone 'cause no woman would tolerate my . . . '

' . . . quirks?' Laura's gentle laughter loosened the knot of tension in his gut. 'We've all got those. I'm not getting into a competition with you.'

'Good. I'd win.' If he wasn't careful, they'd stray away from the subject in hand again. 'Kids.' Hunter grasped her hands. 'I'd love a family. With you. Is that plain enough?' He couldn't spell it out any clearer without taking out an ad in the newspaper. Laura's mouth gaped like a fish, although he wasn't stupid enough to make that comparison out loud. 'I'd prefer to wait until we're a bit further down the line with our plans but if Mother Nature plays around with us, I'm good with that too.' She needed to know he wouldn't let her down. Ever.

'Oh God, I love you so much.'

That swept the legs out from under him because they'd never spelled out their feelings in so many words. 'I love you too.' He gathered her in his arms. 'You've got a choice — dinosaur golf or a hike in the woods. Whatever you want we'll do that. No judgment on my part.'

'You said that with a straight face.'

'Hopefully I'm gettin' better at the whole relationship thing.'

Laura beamed. 'You certainly are, and I'm racing to catch up.'

'Catch me any time you like.'

She squeezed his thigh. 'Let's go walk. I'll easily catch you there.'

'You're on.' In a roundabout way they'd committed to each other and instead of scaring him stiff it had the opposite effect. For two pins he'd suggest they hike up Clingmans Dome, the highest point in the state of Tennessee and shout the good news from the top.

He'd keep that idea tucked away up his sleeve for now.

33

Eight months later — back in the Smoky Mountains

'Remind me again why we're doing this?' Polly gasped and perched on a rock half-way up the steep trail.

'Because you wanted to make the most of this holiday and see everything Tennessee had to offer? My darling boyfriend somehow convinced you this was the best way to round off the trip.' Laura now appreciated the warmth of the new jacket Hunter insisted on buying for her last week because they left behind the mild, autumn temperatures as they started the hike up to the top of Clingman's Dome.

'Are those two idiots racing?'

Their men were striding out in front, almost out of sight around the next wide curve. 'Probably. It's what they do.' Laura tugged her sister back on her feet. 'Come on or we'll meet them on the way down and that would be embarrassing.'

'Not to me it wouldn't. You're the exercise nut these days not me.'

Ever since she returned from her impromptu trip to Tennessee when Hunter's father was ill, she'd made drastic changes to her life. After quitting her hospital job she'd continued to nurse but with a private agency. It gave her the flexibility to accept as many jobs as she needed to pay the bills and the chance to really get to know her patients for a change. With her expanded free time, she'd joined a Dartmoor ramblers' group whose members also took on extended hikes beyond the local area.

'Did I tell you I almost bumped into Mike the other day?'

'Where?'

'In Plymouth.' Polly screwed up her face. 'I crossed the road so he wouldn't see me.'

Hunter had been right. One complaint too many led to it being 'suggested' that he consider leaving the hospital environment for something better suited to his abrasive personality. The pay cut that came along with his new administrative post in charge of a blood testing laboratory was the alternative to losing his medical license.

'He looked in serious need of a haircut and was wearing scruffy jeans and trainers instead of one of his usual budget-busting suits. He's probably strapped for money after paying out a whack each month to Kiki for Demelza.'

'Quite right too.'

'I'm glad you got away from him.'

'Me too.'

'Things are good with Hunter?' Polly probed.

'Yes.'

'Yes? That's all I get?' Her sister griped and struggled to keep up. 'The poor man's visited Plymouth twice in the last six months.'

'I know.'

'He's gone to a therapist like you

302

suggested and could sleep in a pitch-black cave now.'

Laura beamed. 'I'm really proud of him. I know it's been incredibly hard.' She'd helped as much as she could long distance but in the end Hunter had dealt with it all alone. He'd gone through desensitisation treatment that slowly exposed him to dark and confined spaces helping to re-train his brain to behave differently under stress. The therapist spent multiple sessions talking him through the traumas he'd suffered and taught him relaxation and visualisation exercise to use when he became anxious.

'He's not the black sheep of the McQueen family any longer, so what more do you want from him?'

'He's doing everything right, okay?'

'So, what's the problem?'

'There isn't one. Don't rush me.' Laura left her sister to trail along behind and almost walked into Hunter around the next corner. By the rigid set of his jaw he'd heard every word she said.

He struggled to smile but took a wild guess he resembled a dead body with rigor mortis setting in. Last night, after he and Johnny left the women to gossip in the hot tub, they sank a few whiskies and he'd confessed his intention to propose to Laura today. Johnny's only reservation was the timing and now he couldn't help wondering if his friend was right.

'Are we nearly bloody there?' Polly gasped.

'Yep, see that concrete dome that looks like it belongs in a sci-fi movie? That's the observation tower at the top.'

'Thank God. Remind me to ignore you when you talk about going on an easy half mile stroll another time.'

'Let's beat these two to the top.' Laura grabbed his hand. In her challenging stare he picked up an apology, a tinge of worry and more than a hint of a dare.

'You're on.' They raced away and for the next few minutes their speed made breathing a challenge let alone a conversation. Hunter glanced at the people milling around and kicked himself for not realising that on a glorious October day when the leaves were at their peak this place would be overrun. The best he could hope for was to drag her off to one side and pray they wouldn't be interrupted by someone wanting their picture taken.

'My nose is running. Do you have any tissues?'

'Sure.' He fumbled in his pocket for a travel size packet he'd stashed there but something clattered down on the ground. Before he could sweep up the small black box Laura beat him to it.

'Give me that.'

'Say please.' She waved it in the air and made a dramatic play of threatening to open it.

'Please, Laura.' His growling rasp made her lower her arm and thrust the box at him. 'You're makin' this bloody difficult, you know?'

'What you heard earlier, I didn't

mean quite the way it came out.'

'Didn't think so.' He backtracked. 'Well, I wondered for a minute but — '

' — I only wanted to put Polly off the scent. You know me. Here.' Laura rested her hand over her heart.

'Yeah, I do.' Hunter dropped to one knee. 'Marry me.'

'Is that it?'

'I'll throw in more flowery stuff if you want, but I hoped this might do the talkin' for me.' He flipped open the box and the sun set fire to the diamond ring.

'Wow, it certainly does. Yes.'

'Is that it?' Hunter mimicked her and stumbled to his feet. Stuffing the box back in his pocket he grabbed her for a kiss.

Polly and Johnny arrived to join them, and Laura's sister didn't look very happy with her husband. 'He knew.'

'Yeah, he did,' Hunter agreed, 'but — '

' — I warned him it was too soon.'

Polly frowned. 'Laura said a few minutes ago she didn't want to be rushed.'

' — That's only because I didn't want you pestering him! I knew he planned to propose soon.' She looked at him apologetically. 'Sorry, Hunter but you stashed the ring box under your T-shirts and I found it when I was putting away our clean clothes yesterday.'

'So, you peeked and spoiled the surprise!'

'Define spoiled.'

'You don't deny the peeking part?'

'I could.' She shrugged. 'But we don't lie to each other these days so, yes, I did take a quick look.' She wriggled up against him and batted her eyelashes in such an un-Laura like way he couldn't stop laughing.

'I guess it met with your approval, or you wouldn't have said yes.' The words sunk in and Hunter's struggle for breath had nothing to do with the exertion of the hike. 'You said yes,' he whispered.

'I did.' Laura reached into his pocket and pulled the box back out again. 'Is there any chance I get to actually wear this gorgeous ring before I'm old and grey?'

Running his fingers through her pony-tail he pretended to scrutinise her hair. 'I suppose you could've coloured them.'

'What?'

'The grey hairs.'

'Cheeky monkey.' Laura waggled around her ring finger.

Antagonising the future Mrs Hunter McQueen wasn't wise, so he took the hint and slipped the ring on. The simple yellow gold setting matched the glittering flecks in her eyes he'd crazily missed when they first met. 'There. Happy now?'

★ ★ ★

'Very.' Overwhelming emotions swept through her. Joy for the love she'd found with this wonderful man along with a flicker of sadness for the fact her parents would never know him. Laura clung onto him, her rock in an uncertain world. It sounded trite to say they'd always be there for each other but from bitter experience she would never take that for granted.

'Bloody hell, with all this excitement I forgot we've got to drag all the way back down this dreadful hill now,' Polly protested. 'Some engagement celebration this is.'

'Cheer up. It'll give you an appetite for the T-bone steaks and champagne waiting for us at the cabin,' Hunter declared, 'or in your case a hunk of wild Alaskan salmon.'

'Confident, were you?' Laura teased.

'Hey, I can always eat a decent steak and the bubbly would've kept for another time.' His deadpan response made her laugh. 'Last one down is a wimp.' Hunter grabbed her hand. 'Come on.'

Johnny shook his head. 'We're going to take our time.'

'Smart man.' Polly smooched a kiss on her husband's cheek. 'See you down there.'

Laura and Hunter strode offhand in hand. The way it would be from now on.

A few hours later they cuddled up together on the porch with a soft flannel blanket tucked around them to ward off the chill in the air. After wolfing down a delicious meal Polly and Johnny insisted on having an early night and left them alone. Another thing to thank her sister for later.

'More champagne?'

'No thanks, I'm good.'

'Yeah well I know that.' Hunter stroked her face. 'I'd say getting picked up by a cute British babe worked out pretty darn well.'

'I was mad at Polly for lumbering me with some strange American.'

'Yep, for three whole days.' He tweaked her nose. 'Now you're gonna be stuck with me for life.'

She couldn't imagine anything better.

'I'm with you there.'

Understanding and being understood. That's what it was all about. Laura softened into Hunter's kisses as the night wrapped them in its starry embrace. Soon the new day would start.

Thank You

I'm thankful for all of you wonderful people who've read this story and I hope that it was a welcome break away from everyday life. If you've enjoyed Laura and Hunter's story and have a minute to leave a review at the retail site where you purchased your book that would be wonderful.

Angela
x

We do hope that you have enjoyed reading this large print book.

Did you know that all of our titles are available for purchase?

We publish a wide range of high quality large print books including:
Romances, Mysteries, Classics
General Fiction
Non Fiction and Westerns

Special interest titles available in large print are:
The Little Oxford Dictionary
Music Book, Song Book
Hymn Book, Service Book

Also available from us courtesy of Oxford University Press:
Young Readers' Dictionary
(large print edition)
Young Readers' Thesaurus
(large print edition)

For further information or a free brochure, please contact us at:
Ulverscroft Large Print Books Ltd.,
The Green, Bradgate Road, Anstey,
Leicester, LE7 7FU, England.
Tel: (00 44) 0116 236 4325
Fax: (00 44) 0116 234 0205

KISS ME, KATE

Wendy Kremer

When Kate Parker begins work as the new secretary at a domestic head hunting company, the last thing she expects is to fall for her boss! Ryan Hayes, who runs the firm with his uncle, is deliciously appealing. But beautiful and elegant Louise seems to have a prior claim to him, and what man could resist her charms? Plus an old flame makes an appearance in Kate's life. Could she and Ryan have a future together — especially after Louise comes out with a shock announcement?

HER OWN ROBINSON CRUSOE

Susan Jones

Serena Winter normally reports on local events for a travel magazine. Now she's landed her dream job in the Caribbean. On the Atlantic crossing, she's seated next to a grumpy stranger: 'Broderick Loveday, doing nothing and going nowhere,' he tells her. Her job is to report back to 'The Explorer' magazine on drunken monkeys and anything interesting in the islands. The kindness of locals — and someone special — keeps her heart in the Caribbean. But what about when the time comes to leave?

HEART OF ICE

Dawn Knox

Germany, 1938. The escalation of anti-Jewish attacks prompts Kurt's mother to send him to England but when he's boarding the ship, he's mistakenly given a stranger's suitcase. Whilst attempting to return it to its owner, he meets Eleanor but his humble circumstances discourage him from meeting her again. Their paths cross later at RAF Holsmere where Kurt is a pilot and Eleanor a WAAF but is there too much death and destruction to consider taking a chance on love?

ONE GOOD TURN

Sarah Purdue

Fiona will do anything for her best friend, even looking after her trouble-some dog, Archie. When Archie pulls yet another stunt, this time raiding a picnic at the park, she and Archie are rescued by handsome Tom and his impeccably trained dog, Dixon. When Tom offers to help with Archie's train-ing, Fiona can't refuse and finds herself falling in love. But Tom has secrets which threaten their relationship. Can Fiona learn to trust again or risk losing her happy ever after?

LEGACY OF FEAR

Susan Udy

In a desperate bid to escape the scandal and persecution that follow the unexpected death of her husband, Alicia Cornell flees to the small Cornish town of Poltreath in search of a safe haven. But it soon becomes clear that someone there recognises her — and is intent on blackmail. Suddenly, all the people she knows become suspects. Can it really be one of them? And if so, which one? Is her secret about to be exposed, just when she believed she was safe?

CHRISTMAS AT THE GINGER CAT CAFE

Zara Thorne

Jilted at the altar, Isla Marchant isn't feeling very festive this Christmas. So when her aunt and uncle invite her to run their café while they're away, she seizes the chance. Short one member of staff, Harry Anderton turns out to be the perfect solution when he pitches up in a campervan. Then Isla discovers that there are certain seasonal traditions she's expected to uphold in the café. With Harry by her side, can she contain her growing feelings and give the people around her the celebrations they deserve?